Ys

The Fallen

A Fantasy Novella

by

S.C. Vincent

Follow my social media accounts here: https://linktr.ee/scvincent

Please leave a review for this book. Thank you.

© 2022 Spenser Coleman Vincent

ISBN: 979-8-218-02795-7

Special thanks to my Mother, Sandra Vincent, and sister, Naudia Jones, for their help editing the work.

Formatted by Hawks Barrow Press, LLC
hawksbarrow.com

No portion of the publication may be reproduced or transmitted, in any form or by any means, without express written permission of the copyright holder. Names, characters, places, and incidents featured in this publication are either the product of the author's imagination or are used fictitiously. All rights reserved.

Special thanks to my family.

CHAPTER ONE

Dana was running, running away through the stormy dangerous night of the Dracon Lands. She was risking it all to be saved, to escape sin – her home. To save her soul. Panicked, she aimed to be silent, quieter than the trees whipping and crackling from the storm around her. Anything to not raise suspicion of the dragon spirits hiding in the trees and stones. Her feminine frame betrayed her as her ankle twisted on a wet root protruding from the uneven ground – felling her down a muddy ditch, leaving her scraped and bruised. She landed with a yelp and a mouthful of scum as the water below forced through her and stained her blue hair.

The wind quickened. Dana's breath – her very own heartbeat, were both muted by the winds clashing against the vast forest. It was like a suffocating symphony of chaos, and she couldn't find her place in the arrangement. She shuddered as the screams from the dragon's wisps responded to her cry, flying from their homes in the hallows of the nooks and crannies of the dense woods. They spiraled down upon her like a tornado, moments away from a vicious strike.

Dana's arms struggled to pull her up from the terrible tide. She winced as she dug her nails into the wet clump of grass above and tried to pull herself over onto level ground. Yet each attempt was met with failure, and she found herself stuck in the river of mud. However, the spirits struck her one by one and began to zap away her lifeforce. Her instinct to survive at all costs overcame her pain and exhaustion, and she found the volition to pull herself out of the ditch.

The spirits followed as she hobbled along the murky way. She needed to hurry, as the wind was soon to overcome her, and her sight was dimming. Desperate in her search, eventually she came to find a giant tree, hollowed out to the size of a cave. She entered just as the wind had become too great a tribulation.

No rain. No spirits. No burden. She fell to the ground taking deep, rapid breaths. Exhausted, her eyes frantically scanned for any remaining signs of danger. Seeing nothing in the dark, tiredness consumed her.

She awoke drenched with sweat; her dirty clothes sodden from the heat. Quickly she pulled her legs from the entryway; her feet baked from the sun. She held them in great pain, wanting to curse but biting her lip instead. Slowly, she stood upon her heels and looked about the hollowed-out tree. What surprised her was not its tall ceiling, but rather the giant, dotted egg that rested in the middle of the room on a cushion of greens and twigs. Dana had never seen anything like it. She had to back up to get a full view of the egg, her eyes wide in amazement. She stopped though, as soon as she felt the burning of the sun on her back.

She turned around quickly to avoid the pain, but her sun-burnt soles betrayed her. Stumbling back, she fell and hit her head on something hard and heard a loud cracking sound. She sat silently for a few moments in shock, fearing she hurt herself. From behind her came a jet of an orange colored liquid, small at first but then the stream quickly multiplied. She turned around on her scuffed knees to see that she had fallen into the large egg and cracked it with the back of her head.

Desperately she tried to stop the blustering liquid coming from the increasing cracks – she put her hands upon the biggest gaps in a vain attempt at keeping it together, but with every crack closed, another opened. She cried out when the next stream burst upon her face – she didn't want to hurt the egg. She didn't want to kill it. Then she felt a thud against her palm and looked at it in great amazement – a shadow of another hand from inside the egg touched her own, and with this, she backed away. The egg began to pulsate at great rapidity with a bright pink light. Just as fast did the cracks cover entirely until it burst open and from the egg came a wave of orange yolk that enveloped her.

She opened her eyes and found that the orange substance had left her no dirtier. Rather, her clothes (a simple blue dress and cloak), muddy hair, wounds and burns, had all been cleaned and healed after being in contact with the substance. She smiled at the realization. A heavy thud followed, and her mind was brought elsewhere.

From the egg slid out a young man, covered in the slimy orange yolk. Unconscious, he shivered in pain as he tried to breathe. She leapt to him instantly and lifted him onto her lap – opening his mouth and cleaning out what blocked his airway. She then cleaned his eyes and face. He began to calm and breathe normally, sleeping silently upon her. She looked down at him, noticing his gentle, handsome face, almost boyish in its innocence, though he looked to be her same age. His hair, as red as blood, stuck to his forehead until she removed the last remanence of yolk that remained. She comforted him with doting words, "it's okay, it's okay. I won't leave you. I'll protect you. Sleep well," she said as if he were a newborn child. She cradled him silently as time passed by.

He blinked twice and looked up at her with great clarity. She was surprised, not just at his quick revival, but she swore for a moment that his eyes and pupils looked like that of a cat; yet a second glance proved him to be perfectly normal. Nevertheless, swiftly he got up, turned around, stood firm and greeted her with a smile. He stretched out his hand down to her and said, "thank you, may I help you up?" The girl looked up and cautiously held out her hand to his, with her own nervous smile. He grasped it and pulled her up off the ground with one mighty pull and she fell into his arms, where she blushed and quickly pushed him away.

"I'm sorry if I was too rough," the man said. "It seems I don't know my own strength. But I must thank you for helping me out of there. It feels so much better out here." He stood, half nude, only a cloth of sorts covered his waist. He began to stretch and flex, getting used to his new-found freedom. She turned away and felt blood rush to her cheeks.

"You're welcome. But here, take this," she undid the cloak around her shoulder and put it upon him.

"What's this?" He asked as he fiddled around with the long coat.

"Modesty," She quickly replied. "Now, tell me your name. How did you get in that…egg?"

"You saw me as I was – I was born from it. And here I am now, before you. I know nothing else. I have no name. I know what a name is, oddly enough, but I haven't one. You're the closest I have to a parent, perhaps you should name me?"

Deeply confused by his meaning and situation, she instead solved the simplest problem first. "Ru. That'll be your name. Ru the Red, much like your hair. My name is Dana," she expressed herself with much dignity with her hands, nearly curtsying out of habit.

"Ah, Dana the Blue," Ru said with a smile.

"Well enough," Dana followed. "You say you were just born, but babies are born infants from women – small and weak. Unknowing. But you…"

He walked around as he spoke, studying the environment. "I know of the world but nothing of living in it. I can't explain my existence, but neither can anyone else, correct?"

Dana realized there was a certain wisdom in his words and decided to believe his ignorance. As her eyes had fallen during contemplation, quickly they were upon him again as he had walked directly outside and into the sunlight. She jolted towards him.

"No! Ru! Come back!" She held her hand out to grab him but pulled back once the light touched her skin. The sunlight was too intense, too hot. Surely, she thought, he must have collapsed out there.

"What's wrong?" Ru poked his head back in, "aren't you coming?"

"I can't. During the day, the cursed forest turns barren and hot. Anything the light touches is uninhabitable for human life."

"I'm fine. Hm." Ru appeared to be thinking but responded rather quickly. "Here, give me your hand." He grabbed her and pulled her out of the tree and into the sun. She closed her eyes in fear and let out a scream. But after a while, all she felt was Ru's arms around her. Dana opened her eyes and looked up at him. He said to her, "it's okay, it's okay. I won't leave you. I'll protect you."

She looked around and smiled. "How can this be?" She then became instantly embarrassed because she realized that Ru remembered the first things she said to him.

"As long as you're with me, you'll be safe. The curse of this land won't kill you. The promise you made unto me, I, too, share with you. Just don't let go."

"How can you know this?" Dana asked with an astonished curiosity, her hand to her chest and the other holding his.

"I know this like a baby knows to suckle. I told you before, remember? Now come, let's go."

"Wait, let me go back in for a second." She entered the tree and returned to him with a piece of the cracked egg as she held it over her head like an umbrella, "no sunburn."

Together the two walked for a bit with Ru leading the way. Dana was amazed at what had become of the forest during the day. Where she had fallen into a wet ditch the night before, was now red, cracked, dry earth with bits of sand beneath her toes that was occasionally upturned by the wind. All the wooden, lush trees had now become white, fossilized stone. Dana touched a branch in passing, and as soon as she did, it instantly crumbled and fell away. There was no doubt in her mind that without Ru's strange ability she would've had a fate very similar to that tree. However, once she recognized where Ru was leading her, she came to her senses.

"Stop, we can't go this way!" She began to pull him in the opposite direction but found him too sturdy and unable to move.

"Why?" Ru questioned.

"Because this is the way back! The way back to – just follow me!"

"No, I can't. Can't you hear them?" Ru asked plainly.

She continued to pull him, putting all her weight on her heels, "hear what?"

"The bells."

She stopped, exhausted. "What bells? There are no bells around here… Not anymore."

"How strange. But I do hear them. They're calling for me…" He looked off into the distance, from where she had come. Dana sympathized with him, for he had such a sorrowful face.

"Where you want to go is a kingdom, and it's a foul place."

"How so?"

"I can't say," she looked down to the ground.

"Why?"

"I can't tell you why. I wish I could. But there is a reason why I've been trying to escape, why I risked coming into this cursed place."

He took a moment but eventually responded, "I understand. Regardless, I must go to it, but I swear to you, I will keep you safe. Now come."

"No!" She struggled some more, but he wouldn't budge and continued to pull her, "stop! I don't want to go back!"

He stopped, but just as he did, he cupped his hand to his ear as if he heard something in the distance. "Stop moving!" He commanded Dana. Surprised at his forcefulness, she complied once she heard what was coming. He held her close.

Bursting through the fossilized trees came a large, two-legged creature. Its wings spread far as it opened its sharp-toothed mouth and bellowed an intimidating scream. Dana fell on to the ground and shook in fear. Ru seemed unfazed as he stood firm and tall. "Dana, what is that thing? Dana!?"

She awoke from her shock and answered, "a wy-wyvern. It's like a dragon. It's a man-eater!"

The wyvern charged at them with its long, sneering face, ready to make them its next meal. Ru tried to dodge but couldn't move aptly with Dana attached to him. Quickly he grabbed and held her to his chest and fell onto the ground, escaping the monster's jaws just in time. He stood once more, lifting her up as well. She'd realized that she was holding him back, yet she also knew that if she let go, the heat of the sun would kill her. The wyvern turned and charged once more.

Ru searched desperately for a tool – a weapon – but he found nothing around him. And as the wyvern came in, all he could do was hold out his arm to protect Dana. She cried out, fearing the two would perish. Instead, she found Ru to be quite the match for the beast. Although his arm was bitten within its mouth, he too held on to the creature's giant teeth, refusing to let go. The two were at a stalemate since the wyvern hadn't the strength to surpass Ru's own unnatural capabilities. Yet still, she could see Ru was in pain and the blood rushing from his arm and into the creature's mouth was only further driving its bloodlust. Without a second thought she drove the edge of the eggshell she was holding into the wyvern's eye with all her might.

The beast released Ru as it recoiled with a shriek. Ru took the opportunity to go on the offensive and held her in one arm, jumped, and elbowed the brow of the creature with all his strength causing it to fall to the ground. He followed by wrapping his arm around the wyvern's neck and choking it with his wounded forearm. The two struggled greatly as they wrestled on the scorched earth, with Dana being forced along with them. The tighter Ru's grasp, the more he bled, and the greater the creature's convulsions became as it struggled to breathe. After some time, the scaled monster succumbed to its exhaustion and became docile, recognizing Ru as its superior. He let go and the two stood above it as it looked up at them, one eyed, catching its breath.

"What do we do?" Dana asked regarding the creature.

"We take it for a ride," Ru responded with a smile.

As the creature recovered, Ru commanded it to allow them to fly upon its back. It kneeled before the two, allowing them on. Dana was surprised and impressed that the creature followed his instruction, as such animals rarely listen so well. Dana tightly held on to Ru's waist as the two sat upon the wyverns scaled back, preparing for what may. Ru, whose hands rested around the creature's neck, shouted "go!" and the wyvern instantly kicked off from the red, barren ground, and began to run at a great speed. Dana nearly lost her grip and slid off as the force was so unexpected – her blue hair jolting back into the wind; yet she held on to Ru steadfast. The wyverns speed grew and grew until eventually it spread its wings wide, lifted its legs, and the wind took them to the sky. As the creature flapped its mighty wings, it flew higher and higher until Dana's discomfort commanded Ru to even the creature out. The pair sailed just below the thin clouds among an endless azure sky. "Dana," he spoke softly as they were gently soaring now, "open your eyes, quick!"

She struggled, but overcame her fear and opened them wide with amazement. Below the two was a wide forest of red land and white trees, where she could see small little creatures moving about – probably more wyverns going about their day. She peered into the sky and saw others flying as they ate the birds that dared to venture over their land. A magnificent feeling overcame her as she flew through the sky: freedom. She held onto him, and she felt safe. Amongst a wyvern's back, while flying high above, she felt no fear at all. She felt safe. Her worries of home, for just that moment, left her.

"That way!" Ru pointed to his side, "It's green land and I think I see a building of sorts. A tower. I hear the bells coming from there. Is that where you came from?"

"Yes," she said gloomily, "but the bells haven't rung in years, they can't have. How can you hear them?"

Ru redirected the wyvern and they flew for the tower. "Tell me," he asked, "what is the name of this place? Your homeland?"

"Ys," she said, as the weight of the world returned to her shoulders. "It's called Ys."

CHAPTER TWO

The cool grass beneath her feet was a welcome change after her perilous adventure in the rugged Dracon Lands. Outside of the cursed forest, the weather was normal, and she made no hesitation hopping off the wyvern and letting go of Ru's sturdy frame. She understood that whatever mysterious claim that protected him from the curse was no longer needed. But as she left one tragic world behind, it was only to return to a more familiar one, her home. Slowly, she approached the cities brazen gates until she came to a sudden stop.

"What's wrong?" Ru asked, who followed behind like a little duckling attached to its mother.

"Okay – listen," she continued excitedly, "there is something you should know before we go in… I'm the princess!" She closed her eyes as she blurted out the admission.

"Wow! Really?" Ru had a big smile on his face. "That's great."

"You don't mind? You don't think less of me?"

"Why would I?"

Then Dana realized why he wouldn't think much of her status at all – he'd only been alive for hours and knew nothing of the nature of Ys. The truth she couldn't tell him. "No reason," she responded. "Anyways, when we go in there, they're going to take me away; the guards. To see my father most likely. I'm in trouble, you see." She began to pace about the patch of grass alongside the rode that led up to the giant gate that opened to Ys.

"Why?"

"I ran away. I was trying to find someplace else to go and figured the forest at night was my best option."

"Is this place so bad that'd you'd risk your life so? I wonder… This makes me all the more curious."

Dana was frustrated that she couldn't tell him the truth, that the curse cast upon her and the others that knew the truth of Ys did not allow them to speak of it. Whether in speech or text, the curse muted them. Even thinking of doing so numbed her mouth.

"How did you escape?" Ru added, "through the front gate?"

"No, there is a narrow path between the walls and the hills at the back of the tower, but it would take too long to go all the way back there, and especially pointless to sneak back in since they are probably already looking for me... And I need to ease my father's mind of the matter."

"Let us go," Ru began to charge up the hill towards the gate.

"No!" Dana rushed between him and the city, holding out her arms to stop him. "B-before we go, we have to come up with a plan. The only way I'm going back in there is if you stay with me, understand? We promised each other, remember? That we'd protect each other..."

"Right." Ru nodded his head with great determination; quite the opposite of Dana's shy hesitation.

"So, the only way that they'll let you stay with me is if I claim you as my personal guard. Do you understand? A princess is allowed such a thing."

"Me, your personal guard? If that's the case, then it should be no problem."

"But it also means they'll want to know a lot about where I've been and who you are and where you came from. When they ask that, just follow my lead, do you understand?"

"I believe so."

Dana was left quite confused by Ru's answers, she could never tell if he was being purposefully obtuse or if he was simply daft. His earnestness was not a common trait amongst the populace of Ys.

"After you see the city, I'm sure you'll want to leave." Dana continued, "Those bells you say are calling for you, must simply be a ringing in your ears because the carillon of Ys hasn't rung in a decade. Promise me this, that after you find out what happened to the bells of Ys yourself, you'll help me escape once more? If so, I will let you inside the city – they might not allow you in without me since they don't recognize you. If they never saw you leave, they might suspect you as some monster or trick since no normal person can possibly come from the cursed forest; which is at least how they'll see it. Understand?"

"I do, and I promise. Once I'm satisfied, I will help you. I keep my promises."

"Then let us continue."

The two walked up the hill and stood in front of the giant bronze gate that rested between thick walls which surrounded Ys all the way as far as the eye can see. Dana cleared her throat and yelled up to the top of the gate. "HOY!" She shouted with all her might. A moment passed when a groggy eyed soldier peered his head over the edge of the wall and looked down at the two. The soldier disappeared in a hurry.

The sound of a switch being flipped, and several cranking sounds resulted in the gate slowly opening. What awaited the princess and her personal guard were several soldiers lined up in full armor; they bowed to her. "Princess Dana," the soldier in front spoke first "His Majesty wishes to see you immediately. We have orders to take you to him."

"I understand," Dana replied as she walked to them. The soldiers stood and followed behind as she led the way. "This man here, Ru, saved me while I was out. He is my personal royal guard and you are to treat him with the utmost respect. He'll be with me always from now on. Is that clear?" The soldiers did not dare argue, and so Ru followed closely behind her as the two made their way further into the kingdom, following a brick road.

While the others seemed quite familiar with the scenery leading up to Ys, Ru, however, was amazed upon viewing the gigantic tower of Ys up close. He noticed along the road up to the entrance of the tower, that there was very little land surrounding it. And on what land was available, seemed to be crops and animals like cows, pigs, and chickens. He did not see who tended to them, however; just a house along the rocks which were the towers foundation.

As they reached the end of the road, they finally came to the entryway of the giant tower. The building reached all the way to the sky and its tip hid amongst the clouds. The radiant walls of Ys shone brightly from the rays of the sun in all its golden glory. Ru heard the clatter of a thriving civilization coming from the inside, and upon further inspection of the empty spaces of the tower above, he could see people walking about, dancing, playing – an entire civilization in a single, giant extravagant building.

Ru walked up close to Dana and whispered in her ear, as to not allow the surrounding soldiers to hear, "Dana! Is this it? Your kingdom is this building alone? No houses, nor cities? How could such a building even be constructed?" Ru looked about with great wonder as they entered the large arcade which lead on further in.

"Yes, the tower alone is what remains of Ys," Dana explained as she led the group. "However, we do have homes and cities – they exist within the tower. There are sections people take for their own as shelter. And each level of the tower is considered its own city of sorts – the lower you are, the lower the class. You can get higher only if you are favored by my family."

Ru looked around and found a great market thriving with people simply taking what they wanted from the stalls without paying, and then walking away with no recourse. "And what's the benefit to being at the top?" Ru added.

"The closer to the top, the closer you are to God. We're here." Dana stopped in front of a giant door and the soldiers behind her took it upon themselves to open it and allow her and Ru in, with just a few following behind.

"This is a small room," Ru mentioned as he was quite uncomfortable.

"Sir," replied a soldier, "how can you not know? This is an elevator…"

"Excuse him," the princess interrupted. "He's a simple man."

The soldier nodded and pulled on the cog that protruded from the wall. Suddenly, and with great volition, the room vaulted upwards surprising Ru. He found that Dana and the soldiers within were quite used to the feat. After some time, the soldier stopped pulling on the cog, as it wouldn't go any further, and he returned to form, announcing, "we'll be there in a moment." Nearly as soon as he made his declaration, the room came to a sudden stop and shook, until Ru heard something lock into place. The soldiers then opened the door for the two, and Dana told them to leave as she would see her father alone. Dana and Ru exited the elevator and stood in front of a majestically decorated door by themselves. Ru came to the realization that while he knew much of the natural world, newfound inventions seemed to evade the depths of his initial knowledge.

"I'm sorry for what I said back there," she said sincerely with her palm to her brow.

"Sorry for what?"

"I didn't mean you were simple in that way, not really, but if they suspect you then who knows what will happen."

"It's okay," Ru looked at her with a smile. She looked up with guilty eyes. "I forgive you."

Ru had been ordered to kneel on the black and white checkered floor by Dana; as the two faced her father, King Mordred. Ru stole a glance at the man as he sat elevated on a golden chair. An old man whose skin was nearly transparent, except for the liver spots that covered his body. His eyes were also quite strange; placid and gray, they wandered about aimlessly, appearing blind. But he could see, surprising Ru, as he made apparent.

"I'm glad you aren't harmed, my dear Dana. When Dahut first told me you had run away I was beside myself." His voice was weak and strained. From behind the throne came a darkly character, a black-haired girl, seemingly around the same age as Dana, yet not as beautiful. She dressed scantily, seemingly without shame, as she stood next to her own father. The soldiers in the room took particular notice of her, Ru could tell as they all turned their heads. One soldier, who stood closest to the girl that Ru assumed to be Dahut, took the most pleasure upon her reveal, as he knelt before her. He was also black-haired, his locks waved down to his shoulders, as broad as they were. He was strong and tall – yet, before her, meek and small. His eyes were fixated upon her in the most possessive of ways.

The girl spoke, "sister, where were you? It reflects so badly on our poor father when even his own daughter tries to run away. Doesn't it, father?"

"Yes, Dahut." There was a slight delay in his response, Ru noticed. A monotone dullness laced the King's cadence.

"Father, shouldn't she tell us where she went and why?"

"Y-yes, yes she should, Dahut."

Dana looked fiercely at her sister from across the room and replied surprisingly calmly, "Oh, father, my king, it is true what *she* says. I ran away, yet again."

"But this time you managed to leave the city's gates." Dahut continued, "how?"

"No one dares question a princess, isn't that right, sister?"

Dahut smirked and replied, "indeed. Continue, where did you go? Out there, out where there is surely nothing for you?"

"I went into the woods."

"The cursed Dracon Lands!?" Dahut exclaimed with a fakeness even Ru could notice. "Why, sister, would you dare venture to such a dangerous place? Are you suicidal? Must we lock you up for your own safety?"

"Father," Dana replied, not acknowledging her sister, "I was a fool, true. I found the woods to be quite hazardous and so I returned home. My curiosity simply got the better of me – I shan't do it again. Please forgive me, your dearest daughter."

Dahut returned to her fathers' ear and whispered to him. The king spoke plainly, "young man – you with the red hair. Stand before me." Ru approached and faced the room – the knight across the room looked at him quite bitterly and Dahut very inquisitively. Ru noticed Dana's nervous glances towards him, seemingly worried at how he'd handle the questioning. "Lad, what is your name? Who are you and why are you here?"

"King of Ys, my name is Ru the Red. I am here as the Royal Guard of Princess Dana."

"Oh! Dana, when did you finally decide to take a guard like your sister?" The king pointed to the dark-haired knight standing close to Dahut.

"He saved me from the woods, father," Dana replied. "He's the only one worthy since he risked his life to enter such a dangerous place to rescue me."

Dahut interrupted, "he saw you enter the woods, at night?"

"Yes."

"You, Ru, was it? Don't I know you from somewhere?"

"No…?" Ru answered Dahut.

"Hm, tell us your tale of heroism, so we know how to thank you properly."

"My guard does not answer to you," Dana replied abruptly. "And I have not given him permission to do so."

"But I believe father would like to know as well, the man who saved his daughter's life, and reward him properly. Right, father?"

"Yes, Dahut." The king's voice became flat once again.

Dahut looked down at Dana with a smug grin, and so, Dana ordered Ru to reply, "tell them, Ru, how you saved me…"

"We met in the woods and were confronted by a wyvern. Together, we defeated it and returned to Ys. That is all."

Dahut's brow furrowed as if her mind stirred with great suspicion, nevertheless, before she could continue, the king interrupted.

"Oh my! You faced one of those wretched things and survived?"

"Yes, as you can see from the blood on my arm that we did not go unscathed. However, I did not let any harm come to the princess."

"You were right to make this man your royal guard, Dana. Any who dare risk his life against such a foul beast is most worthy. It is such an honorable feat."

Dahut's guard fixated on Ru with a vicious gaze.

"Thank you, King of Ys," Ru replied.

"Father," Dana interrupted, "now that I have explained myself, can I go? I would like to return to my room and rest."

Before the king could respond Dahut spoke for him, "no! You cannot! You broke fathers' rules again and hurt his feelings. He worried for you. And for that you must be punished."

Dana grew fierce, "it is not your place, Dahut! You are *not* the King! It was not father who made those rules -" Suddenly, Dana's mouth shut violently, and her lips grew twisted and closed. Ru found this to be quite strange. The princess looked to be trying to say something, but it seemed her body was fighting against her! This greatly worried him, and he would have gone over to her if she had not held her palm out, which he interpreted as for him to keep away.

"Father!" Dahut shouted. "Don't you agree that she should be punished for running away to the Dracon Lands? For hurting your feelings so? For making you look weak to your people?"

"Yes, Dahut," the King replied yet again.

"Take her to the dungeon for the night."

"No!" Dana cried as the soldiers surrounded her, beckoning her to follow. She did so reluctantly as she looked back at Ru who followed behind.

"Stop! You, Ru," Dahut shouted. "You are to stay here. The king wishes to speak with you alone."

"No. I will be with Dana. I promised her." The other soldiers in the room began to move towards him as they prepared to act on possible orders.

"You will stay," the King spoke.

Dana walked through the soldiers and whispered to him in his ear. He nodded, and she then left the room with the troop, leaving him alone.

Dahut commanded Ru once more, "although my father would like to speak to you, the blood on your body is unsightly and offends him. These soldiers here will take you to your new quarters as a royal guard, where you shall bathe. Then, you will be escorted back here." The princess returned to her father's side once more.

Ru examined the room as the guards surrounded him and asked him to follow. He could feel the hatred coming towards him from Dahut's royal guard. He saw how Dahut's fingers danced atop her fathers' throne as he sat there, looking about aimlessly. She wore but one ring, he noticed, on her right-handed ring finger and it was a crowned lavish jewel. Something about the situation felt greatly wrong to him. He followed the guard and exited the room.

He sat in the warm, bubbly bathtub as the lilac soap soaked away any dirt, grime, or blood that stained his fit body. He felt uncomfortable in the large room, for he was nude and surrounded by servants that stood nearby in case they were ordered by him to fulfill some command. He had told them to leave, instead, they stood afar and turned away.

While scrubbing his body clean, his mind wandered on about the strangeness of Ys, *'there must be something more as to why Dana ran away. Why can't she tell me of Ys' supposed evils? And a kingdom usually has cities, and castles, not just one single giant tower. Especially one so big. At least, that's what comes to mind. It seems I know of some things but not of others... It's like I'm incomplete.'* He dipped his head under the water to clean his hair and came up feeling quite refreshed. *"To be closer to God'...that's what Dana said. I don't know anything about that.'* He leaned back into the tub, finally being able to relax as he was lost in confusion. *'Her sister and father, something isn't right about them either. The King seemed caring one second but always in Dahut's favor the next. Regardless, I must protect Dana. I will see to her tonight when nobody is around, like she told me, but before that, I need to find those bells. They've only gotten louder since I arrived.'*

Suddenly the servants shifted about and exited the room. Ru looked about, splashing some water onto the floor. He could feel something was wrong. From behind one of the pillars came Dahut. She wore a small towel and a confident smile with a matching strut that demanded his attention. She stopped before the tub, dropping the cloth, exposing her bare body, and glared at him inquisitively. Ru looked away with a sudden urgency and immediately set to get out – until she dipped her toes into the water and joined him in the tub sized for one.

"You seem so familiar, yet you serve my sister. Wouldn't you rather serve me? I doubt she's the type to let you do this. You could have all of this," she caressed her breasts, "and more. I hold more influence than her – more money, more women. With me, you could have anything." Her toes underneath the water met a dangerous place as her hands slid up from his shins to his knees. "All you have to do is leave her for me. What do you say? Come here," she pushed out her chest, "come to me, and I'll give you all you desire."

Ru jumped out of the tub onto the tiled floor and looked down at her with great disgust.

"Are you rejecting me? I would think twice, fool. I could have the guards in here any moment and claim you tried to force yourself on me and have you executed on the spot!" Dahut's eyes found their way down to explore his bare form. Her eyes widened at what she saw, "your forearm – what exactly happened to it?"

Ru looked down at his arm. Now that the blood was washed away, he found it to be fully healed and strangely covered by scales. "My arm? I got bit by the wyvern." He didn't understand why the parts where he was bit looked that way – like that of the body of the wyvern itself, he was just as surprised as she was, perhaps more.

"Perhaps you are not who I thought you were." Dahut stood up and got out of the tub with a suspicious gaze upon him. She turned away and left the room, paying no mind to her nudity.

Ru was left alone with new concerns but hadn't the time or means to find any answers. The king awaited him. He clothed himself in the provided long-sleeve, white shirt and brown pants, and left the large bathroom. Walking down a few halls, he found his way back to the door to the throne room where the king awaited; but was stopped by the guards.

"Halt! You are not to enter."

"No, the king asked to see me after I was cleaned. I am Ru, Dana's royal guard. Let me through."

"We were given new orders. You will return tomorrow. He will see you then. Leave now." The guard pointed Ru towards the elevator.

He entered it and made his way down to the base of Ys. The entire time down, he couldn't help but wonder who gave them those new orders.

CHAPTER THREE

The city streets called to him as he wandered about the never-ending circular avenue. Ys was wrapped in layers of walls; on the most outer layer of streets one could easily walk about in the sunlight. The streets and walls themselves were made of the highest quality of stone. They were extremely dense, impossibly strong, and painted in gold. However, the further Ru walked into the depths of the streets the more they became like a maze. The further he went, the more artificial the light became, with dimly glowing, odd stones that adorned the halls. As he continued, the more difficult the roads became to navigate. The streets filled with the poor and suffering bothered him to no end, finding that the further into the center of Ys he went, the stranger the atmosphere became.

On the outer layers of Ys, the people seemed relatively normal - personable. But the further in he went, the more callous and ambivalent they were. Ru walked about the populace as they wandered from building to building. He walked past a building that smelled foul, and out came bumbling men and women, unable to walk straight and slurring their words. One chubby patron bumped into him and looked to start a fight. The man swung his fist and missed, Ru responded with a slight push and the man fell to the ground, falling asleep soon after. Ru found almost everyone to be intoxicated to some degree with some sort of drug.

The men were lecherous and women loose, dressed provocatively and without shame, there was no concern of public displays of affection even if children were present. Sickened, Ru stopped in his tracks and noticed a thick essence in the air – a smoke that worsened his condition. Yet it seemed none of the others in the vicinity were bothered by the polluted air. Ru heard shouting in the distance from the front of a brothel, "you little shit! Bring me a drink, now." An old man kicked a small, gangly pointed-eared creature after he commanded it. The thing rolled all the way to Ru and looked up at him – its wrinkled, leathery face looked up at him in great fear and ran to the shadows. It reappeared with a drink and, taking extra care to avoid Ru, delivered it to the drunkard.

The creature's presence filled Ru with a great disdain. Something about it disgusted him and filled him with great hatred – but now he noticed that these small, two-foot-tall creatures were just about everywhere, at the service of anyone who called for them. They kept to the shadows with a wry grin and fulfilled every selfish demand the citizens requested. However, they all seemed very aware of Ru's presence and avoided him diligently.

Ru had come to find himself at the center-most point of the tower on the base floor and found that up just a few steps was a giant, wooden door. He found his eyes transfixed by the entryway, and by the black miasma emanating from it. As a cold sweat began to drip from his brow, a woman bumped into him from behind.

"Sorry," she said with a smile. She held her infant child in her hand. "Pardon, I mustn't be late."

Ru nodded and let her by. She climbed up the stairs, opened the creaking door, and the two entered the dark room. Ru couldn't see much of what was inside from where he was standing. He decided to follow the woman. Up the steps he went, although slower than her, his nerves were beginning to weaken, and his legs began to shake. He couldn't understand why, but by the time he was atop the few steps, he found himself to be crawling on his hands and knees. He stood once more and reached out to the door – everything about him was telling him to leave. He couldn't find the strength to push the door open.

Suddenly, the woman he'd met just moments before exited the building and met him with a smile. "Nice to see you again," she said to him in passing. He noticed as she walked by that she no longer carried her child. He walked through the opened door and into the darkness. There was very little light. *'Where did she leave the child? Perhaps a nursery? In here?'* He thought to himself. He continued to walk forward until his next step found no ground and he nearly fell. His reflex caught him, and he fell back. It took some time before his eyes could adjust, but once they did, he realized something.

Before him was the innermost room of Ys, it was vacant all the way to the top and bottom. There were no other rooms, just doors of the other levels above him. There was no nursery. Before him was a giant, endless pit with a darkness that nearly engulfed him. His eyes bulged, and throat tightened, while his pulse filled his head. His breath had left him as he leaned over the edge and peered into the dark – something evil was calling to him, something at the bottom. He nearly joined it.

The sound of bells came to him again and broke him free of the curse. Ru ran from the room and dashed out from the smoky bellows of Ys into the shallowest parts where the sun's rays touched the stone; where people were most sane. He fell onto the ground, curled into a ball, and in great despair, he realized where the woman had left her child.

Ys, he'd come to realize, was not what it seemed.

"Where am I?"

Ru sat up slowly, analyzing the strange, cluttered room. Surrounded by various mechanical devices and heaps of metal, he stood up from the thin, uncomfortable cot asking the question again to the old man across the room. "You, sir, where am I? The last thing I remember…"

The man, looking to be in his sixties, stood up from his drawing table and walked towards him. He was short but in good shape for someone his age. He was always in a hustle and in a constant sweat. Oil and grease filtered his burnt skin and his hands were calloused from what must have been decades of hard physical labor. His unkempt mustache danced above his lips as he spoke, "you're not from around here, are you? You can't fool me! I knew the moment I saw you blubbering on the floor. My name is Peter, by the way." The old man held out his rough hand to Ru, who grabbed it and shook firmly.

"Thank you, I suppose," Ru replied. "I lost myself for a moment."

"More than a moment, you've been asleep all afternoon. The sun is beginning to set. You got a place to stay?"

"Yes… What is this place?"

"My home," Peter walked to the fire pit across the way, which occupied a dim flame. Above it hung large, metallic buckets attached to the high ceiling. "If you could call such an unwelcoming place that." Peter grew silent as he looked across the grungy room at all the tools and oddly shaped iron objects. "Follow me," Peter led Ru out of his home and to the fields that surrounded the great tower of Ys.

"These are my fields. I grow my own food out here – what I can at least. I don't like to rely on those damned korrigans, the little bastards."

"Those small creatures that hide in the shadows?"

"Yeah, they provide all the food and do all the labor for us here. Leaving us like sloths."

Ru looked about the great flourishing fields, "I remember this. When I was walking up there," Ru pointed to the road some ways away that led from the entrance to the tower. "I saw these grand plants, but I saw no one tending to them."

"It takes most of my time. But today, I've been in my room racking my brain over something." Peter spit on the ground and shooed a chicken away.

"What would that be?"

"The same thing I've been trying to remember for the last ten years. It's been my burden… But never you mind, where do you come from? I could tell only a stranger would be so overcome by what's within the tower – only virtuous men grow sickly from it. And there are none of those left."

"I'm from the Dracon Lands."

Peter's eyes grew large, "impossible – no one can live in that hazardous place. It's cursed for us humans."

"Right…" Ru looked downward and held his right arm. "Dana found me in an egg and together we escaped and came here. But I think maybe I was wrong in bringing her back."

"You know my little Dana!?" Peter grabbed Ru's arm desperately. "What happened? Is she okay? They don't let me see her anymore."

Ru backed away and sat on a tree stump behind him, "they sent her to the dungeon for the night for running away. I brought her back to Ys because I needed to investigate the ringing of the bells. But now I realize that it was a mistake. This is no place for the innocent. People like her and the children I see wandering about in the streets. I'm sure they're orphans…" Ru, in great dismay, brought his palms to his face.

"You heard the bells? The bells of Ys?" Peter's voice was littered with doubt.

Ru looked up unexpectantly at the man's reply, "Yes! Can you!?" He stood swiftly and approached the man, "can you hear them as well?"

"Come with me," Peter responded, "and I'll explain what I can."

The two walked up the brick road to Ys, but instead of walking into the building they walked around it. As tall as the tower was, it was proportionally just as wide, causing them to take several minutes to reach their destination as they strolled among a declining path. Ru noticed the fields Peter tended sloped into water, and the walls surrounding Ys ceased as the ocean behind Ys came into view. It was a long walk so Ru attempted to fill the silence with a bit of conversation, "how do you know of Dana? Outside of her being a princess, of course."

"A long time ago, we worked in the church together, back when she was a child. We grew very close. She was the closest I had to a daughter. And with her father, the king, ever so busy, I believe I was something like an uncle to her. But Dahut doesn't like us seeing each other anymore."

"She seems to have a lot of influence… Tell me, does Dana have any other family she can rely on?"

"None. Her mother passed away when the two children were young and her uncles died long ago, along with her grandfather, King Arthur. She's been alone most of her life. That's why I've always tried my best to be there for her."

"I see…" A sorrow overcame Ru and the two became silent once more.

A half-hour passed and they arrived fully behind the building and to a giant pier that went out into the calm, blue ocean. Firstly, however, Peter pointed out the giant door behind them. "I'm sure you can tell, young man, that a great power resides behind this door," Peter explained.

"It's similar to what I felt when I peered into the hole at the center of Ys. I can smell, and even see a dark miasma coming from the cracks of the door."

"You can? I cannot. Hm, regardless, yes, that's the bottom of the pit. Follow me," Peter beckoned Ru on as the two walked down the pier and further into the ocean. "I hope you can understand that there are things Dana and I wish to tell you but cannot. Do you understand what I mean, lad?"

"I believe I do. Dana mentioned something about the carillon not ringing for a decade and you've mentioned a similar time frame, as well. Something happened to this place ten years ago, something that caused a great evil to overtake the kingdom. It's the same thing that doesn't allow its citizens to speak the truth of what happened." The two continued down the pier until they came to its end.

Peter continued, "I believe you fully now, about where you said you're from. Nobody from Ys could say what you have just said. Dana, as a young girl, was the purest and holiest of maidens. She dedicated herself to the Lord, attended church every Sunday, and volunteered in any function that she could. Through that, her handmaiden, Julia, a former nun, grew very close. Although Dana was the younger sister, she outshined Dahut in every way possible. The people looked up to Dana and loved her dearly. This made Dahut bitter, and entrenched with hatred and jealousy. I know this because I am a man of faith, as well. I operated, even created, the carillon that hung in the bell tower of the church. But as you know, something happened ten years ago that stopped us all from attending church and…caused the bells to stop ringing. That part is my fault and if I had kept them ringing then none of this… Well, that is the extent of how specific I can be on the subject."

Peter pointed down into the ocean and what Ru saw left him flabbergasted. Through the clear blue ocean, Ru could see the remnants of a great civilization – a vast underwater city once inhabited by the populace of Ys; now a sodden state littered with fish, coral, and seaweed. An underwater ghost town. Ru now realized that the city that once inhabited the canyon below was the true Ys, not the tower. Ru staggered about as he viewed the world beneath him and became unbalanced. The water was so clear that a strange vertigo overcame him as he feared he might fall straight through to the bottom.

"Calm down, lad," Peter held him in place to ground him.

"Sorry. You're right. I haven't felt well since I entered the tower. What happened to it, the city?"

Peter's lips began to move but nothing audible came out. He simply looked at Ru with a hurt smile. "All I can say is this," he pointed downwards at a specific point in the water, to a very large cathedral that lay in ruins, "that is where the ringing you hear is coming from. They are the only bells in existence in all of Ys."

"How can you be so sure?"

"That's what I've been trying to do for the last ten years – remember how to make the bells. But once *it* happened, the knowledge of how to make them simply left my mind. A stolen memory. You saw the equipment in my home and the drafts on my desk, I've tried to make a bell foundry. Throughout the years I've been trying to put two-and-two together, but every time I think I get close, the solution seems to get further away. Like a carrot on a stick."

Ru knelt to the water, introspectively looking at his reflection. "Then why can only I hear them…and why do they ring? How?" He held out his hand, dipping it in. Peter jumped at him and pulled him from the water's edge as fast as possible.

"Don't! Stop, look!" The two looked down into the underwater city once more and out came hundreds of humanoid aquatic creatures. They swam deftly up from the houses to the oceans top with weapons such as rusted tridents, spears, and swords in hand. Quickly, the once gentle sea turned to a wave of terminal threat. The creatures - brown, blue, or red - looked up at Ru with their giant, bulbous eyes and scaled skin with webbed appendages. They pointed their weapons at him, ready to strike. Yet he stood firm. "Quick, run!" Peter took off back down the pier, "they don't go towards the door!" Ru heard him yell from behind.

Ru, more curious than cautious, held out his hand to the closest of the finned threats and upon his touch, the fear and anger that filled its cloudy, spherical eyes vanished and it retreated below to whence it came; as did the others.

"H-How did you do that?" Peter asked. "Those damn mermaids kill everyone that touches the water. That's why nobody dares come back here, nevertheless build a boat."

"I don't know. It seems there is a lot I don't know. But when I saw them, I wasn't afraid, rather, I felt great sympathy. It was like when the bells call to me, I needed to get to it – to touch it. So, I touched him, and he felt peace. I can't explain it any further."

"Neither can I. Maybe they're the ones ringing the bell, all the way down there. Calling you. Maybe not. All I can say is, I have faith in you, lad. It seems we both want the same things. If you ever need me, you know where I am." Peter turned away and continued up the path towards his home.

Ru stood at the pier for a few moments looking into the water, noticing now that the ringing had stopped.

He spent the rest of the daylight playing ball with the orphaned children that wandered the streets of Ys.

The evening moon outshone all of the stars in the dainty, blue sky. Dana could just barely see it through the street gutter above, having been imprisoned in the sewer cell beneath the roads of the second floor of the tower. What little moonlight that did sneak through illuminated the dank dungeon in which Dana resided. It was like a spotlight posed to expose her deceit and loneliness. The only thing keeping her company throughout the day was the sound of the footsteps of passerby's above as they happened to kick dirt into the small chamber below. She sat alone on a cold, stone slab, devoid of thought or feeling. Her faith in Ys had begun to waver in recent times. Her faith in herself as well. She was shocked as the bars of the gutter came crashing in, making a loud clinking sound as the iron fumbled across the floor.

No sooner did she scream that Ru slid his way through the narrow hole and landed on the ground. The moonlight embraced him from behind, encircling him with a bright aura. She was taken by his beauty, angelic as it was. He moved out of the way and sat next to her.

"I'm sorry I'm late," he pleaded. "It seems we've both had a terrible day."

"It's okay, I told you to come later on after all. If the guards had seen you, they might have tried to imprison you as well. But do tell me, what happened with your meeting with my father?" Dana looked up at him with a desperate curiosity.

"I'm sorry," Ru continued, "a beautiful bird shouldn't be caged like this. I'll never let this happen to you again, I promise. I'll tell you all about it tomorrow, but now rest."

Although she recognized her exhaustion and was taken by his pleasant words, she didn't want to listen. She wanted to act. "Sleep? Where? There is no place to rest my head. I want to know what happened, was it that bad?"

"Shh," Ru calmed her. "Rest your head here," he motioned to his lap.

"No! That's…unseemly!" She scooted away to the edge of the stone slab.

"You once did the same for me when I was weak and tired. I'm merely returning the favor. You needn't worry, I mean nothing more by it. I am tired as well, but I have a stronger constitution than you and can manage sleeping while sitting up. As your guard and friend, let me make the night easier for you."

Slowly she approached him; a warmness to her cheeks, she rested her head on his strong, firm thighs. Although a proper princess should never have done this, and she felt completely wrong doing it, she also felt safe with him and trusted him entirely. It didn't take long for the two to fall asleep.

The day had been poor and long, but the night short and sweet.

CHAPTER FOUR

"I can't believe him!"

Dana threw her clothes across her bedroom as she picked apart her wardrobe, finding nothing to her liking. Her handmaiden, Julia, wandered from place to place, picking the clothes up from the floor. Dana had always known her to be a kind and reverent woman, who always helped her when she could, whether with services or advice. Not only was she handy with stitching torn clothes, but she was also competent in nursing practices. Dana continued her fit, "I can't believe he let her do that! He makes me so angry."

"Princess," Julia replied, "from what you told me, it seems that he didn't invite the matter. Your sister seemed to be taking advantage of him."

Dana turned around, donning a damp towel around her torso. Her blue hair snapped droplets of water across the wall. "But don't you think as a man he should've acted sooner? Told her off beforehand? Maybe he wanted her."

"My dear sweet Dana, come here," Julia sat on the Princess' bed and patted it, beckoning the girl over. Dana sighed, hesitating at first, but followed suit. "From what you've told me about him, he's not a normal man. You said he's only about a day old, although I find that difficult to believe. How was he to know what to do in that situation? How was he to know better? What matters is he rejected her advances and stood by your side. Look, my dear, you shouldn't be so mad at him, it's obvious he felt bad about it or else he wouldn't have told you. The fact that he did means he's a good man and cares for you."

Dana looked down in deep thought, moving her toes across the fine rug on the floor. "I...guess you're right."

"But what I think is most interesting, my little princess, is how you've misplaced all your anger onto him and not towards your sister."

"What do you mean?"

"He's *not* your sister. He's not the one who betrayed you. Do you, perhaps, have feelings for the boy?"

"What!?" Dana got up and stepped away. "Of course not! How could I? I've only just met him. And – and I'm a princess and he's…"

"The only good man you've ever known."

Dana looked away from Julia, flustered and confused. She returned to her wardrobe.

"You're eighteen, an adult, Dana. It's okay to have those feelings." Julia paused but Dana didn't reply, as she continued to go through her clothes. "He seems to be your same age, at least his body does. It's okay to acknowledge those feelings, acting on them, however…"

"I'm ready." Dana turned around fully clothed. Her attire matched her intentions; her walking boots and green, skin-tight pants proved that she was serious about her plans. Over her white long-sleeved shirt, she wore a brown leather vest that tied around her waist. Her shoulder pads were prominent but not so much as to get in her way. They, along with the vest, acted as a sort of armor.

"In that? Your outside clothes? You're just going to see your father, unless you're planning to…"

"You know why I left, Julia. I failed once, but with Ru, I think I can do it. I can find help. He told me he met Peter. Now he knows everything that we could possibly tell him."

"You haven't seen Peter in quite a while, have you?"

Dana shook her head as she headed for the door to the hallway.

"Dana, remember what I said about the boy… And don't forget this, it's your favorite." Julia handed Dana a necklace that she inherited when her mother, the queen, passed away. It was a simple, silver chain with a bird adorning it.

Dana gave a reassuring smile, put the necklace on and left the room. There Ru stood, diligently waiting by the door in the hallway for her. "Your hair's still wet. You'll catch a cold," he noted.

"Follow me," she replied as she walked down the hall to the throne room.

"Look, I'm sorry. You're still upset, aren't you? She threatened me, what else could I do?"

Dana stopped and looked at him. "When we first met… I don't want you to think I was simply running away from home, like some spoiled little girl."

"What?"

"I was trying to find a solution to…" Dana struggled to find the correct words she could use that the curse upon her wouldn't censor, "the problem that ails Ys. If you understand what I mean."

"Now I do, yes. The evil that infected Ys ten years ago; the curse on those who dare to speak on its details, and the reason why the people are so fallen."

"That's why after we're done talking with my father I want to try again. And I want you to come with me. I… I can't do it without you."

"The bells ring no more. Ys is no longer calling out to me now that I know what it wants. I think you and I want the same thing – to save it. To bring her back to how she was – for the pure and innocent. And I think you're tied to its fate inexorably. To save Ys, I must save you. Of course, I will go with you."

She smiled and the two continued down the hall and stopped just before the giant doorway to the throne room, where they saw Dahut standing angrily in front of the guards, demanding to be let in. Her royal guard, the black-haired man with the fierce eyes stood calmly by her side; until he noticed Ru's presence. His posture stiffened and his upper lip became crooked.

"Move aside you cretons! I am Princess Dahut – you serve me! If I wish to be with my father I will be!"

"Sorry, My Highness," the guard in front of the door explained, "but the King gave us strict orders to allow only Princess Dana and her royal guard into the throne room."

Dahut looked back towards Dana and Ru as they arrived and quickly composed herself. "Ah, dear sister, it seems you are the most beloved after all. Both by father…and by your guard!" She laughed as she and her royal guard left in a hurry down the hall.

Dana hated her sister. After years of abuse, she no longer felt guilt towards accepting that fact. "Nothing happened!" Dana shouted, wanting to clear the record about the previous night's events. That morning, when the guard on duty came to let her out of the cell, he found the two sleeping together. Dana cared not about what her sister thought of her, but more so of what the guards thought and how fast rumors can spread throughout the kingdom. Although Dana knew her virtue led her to be unpopular in current times, she still believed in the morality the old church instilled in her. She also knew just how lecherous some of the guardsmen and knights could be if given the opportunity – a nature her sister nurtured in them.

The guards opened the mighty doors and the two followed in as the old king welcomed them in with a thin smile. As the doors began to shut, he ordered the remaining guards and servants to leave the room, leaving just the three of them. The closing of the door reverberated through the large hall and suddenly, her father's smile turned to pouting, blubbering lips as he jolted from his throne and hobbled as fast as he could to his daughters' side, kneeling before her. His crown had fallen from his head as he'd come forward and Ru left her side to retrieve it from the floor. Dana looked down at her teary-eyed father and looked up at Ru once more. She was desperate and looked to him for an answer as to what to do. He offered none. She'd never seen her father act in such a way, even in the worst of times.

"D-dana! Thank God you came back home to me! The thought of being left alone with – with!"

"Dahut?"

"Yes! She's horrible, she controls me. I can't stop her and when I try, she hits me – look!" The frail king opened his shirt to reveal his torso and what looked to be several purple and blue bruises all over. "Please, please save me from my daughter!"

Dana knelt to her father and gave him a soft hug. She whispered to him, "of course, father, I'll help you. But what took so long for you to tell me? I've known…" The curse stopped her from stating explicitly Dahut's true nature. "I've known how she is. All you had to do was come to me. I would've helped. Why haven't you before?"

Ru moved in and slowly helped her father up onto his legs and returned his crown to his head. "Thank you, young man. Dana, my dear, the reason why is because you wouldn't be able to do a thing. She…is the true ruler of Ys. My mind and body are weak and with her sway with the people, I have very few men loyal to me. I am just a figurehead, to be used until I die. At which time she will take over as queen and be welcomed by the citizens with open arms. Yet if I die an unnatural death, her reign will always be suspect, and her power weakened. Already the people, the guards, knights, all love her…her debauchery. If you acted, if you had tried to stop your sister, she would have executed you in some way."

"Why now?" Dana persisted, "what's changed?"

The king pointed towards Ru. "When I heard you left, truly left, I felt so scared. So alone. All this time your fighting spirit is what's kept me going, hoping you'd be the one to stop her. And then you were gone." The king looked towards Ru, "it's him. Knowing he has the strength to fight a wyvern and survive the cursed forest – I knew he must be the one that can help free us from this evil. You must be blessed in some way! Thank the Lord for you, my boy! Since I met you yesterday, I've ordered to be alone. I've been trying my best to keep her away so we could meet alone. Dear, I'm sorry I put you in the dungeon yesterday, if I hadn't, she…"

Dana was immensely confused by her father's reasoning but hadn't the time to question it, "I understand, father, it was fine. I was comfortable."

"Good." The king directed his attention towards Ru once more, "Ru, was it? Come with me, there is something I must ask of you. Come, alone."

"What? Father, anything you can say to him you can tell me. He's my royal guard after all."

"He might just be our civilizations savior, as well. Now, please."

Dana ceased to protest and watched them as they walked into the king's bedroom – Ru turned his head and looked at her as the door shut. She picked up a goblet next to her father's throne, sprinted across the marble floor, and placed it on the thin wall. She leaned into the cup and listened to their conversation.

Ru instantly noticed the stale stench from the dusty room – he stopped himself from sneezing several times as the king led him across the surprisingly sparse space. Besides the messy four-post bed, which was dutifully kingly sized, and topped with a carefully woven blanket, nothing else littered the floor and walls of the lacking room. Besides the bed, there were almost no other signs of the room being in use. The king led him across the soft floor to his desk where a thick, black book awaited them. It was no insignificant thing; for the king struggled to lift it.

"Here," King Mordred pushed the book into Ru's hands, "open it."

Ru felt his palms begin to itch and then burn from the touch of the black, bound tome. He let it go and it fell to the ground. The king's eyes widened as it fell, and he jolted faster than Ru had ever seen him move to pick it up from the floor.

"How dare you! Be more careful – this is the holy text. The Bible! The only copy… I wanted you to look through it, not drop it!"

"Sorry."

"It's all right. Here, look, I'll show you," Mordred opened up the Bible on the desk and showed its pages to him. Ru was surprised that the book featured no text at all, the entire scripture was told in drawings – artwork that described a story.

"What is this?" Ru asked, "What is this book about?"

"This book details the true history of Ys and what happened to it ten years ago. It is the only copy in existence and has remained hidden since it was given to me by a priest who has long since passed. I'll tell you its story." The king began to flip through the pages while explaining the events. "This here is God, you can see Him giving us divine plans along with those little creatures, the korrigans."

Ru saw the depiction of God as a black creature with the head and legs of a goat, with horns, hoofs, and long ears. It also featured the torso of a gorilla, with its burly strong arms. Its tail was long and thick with the tip being an anaconda's face. Wings like that of a bat were attached to its back. It towered over the men drawn on the page as it handed over the written directions.

King Mordred continued, "God wanted us, His children, to return to Him, thus He gave us those instructions on how to build this tower. He provided us with those korrigans - His angels, to aid us in its construction, as well as to make our lives easier until we completed the tower, as you can see here," the king pointed to what resembled the tower of Ys, "until we met Him back in Heaven upon the towers completion." The drawing the king pointed at lastly portrayed God sitting on his throne in the clouds along with mankind, happily dancing around Him, worshiping Him. "In Heaven, there is no worry, no age. Just happiness."

"So, what happened next? Obviously, this didn't come to be." Ru urged the king to continue his story.

"This." Mordred turned the article and what filled the next two pages was a fiercely drawn image of a giant dragon fighting the goat-faced God, deathly injuring Him. "My daughter Dahut became possessed by the Devil, this dragon. He promised her the world – all of Ys and more as long as she willed him into the earthly realm."

"And how did she do that?"

King Mordred turned the page, depicting giant walls that once surrounded Ys. "The Devil, also known as Satan, needed a significant sacrifice. In her foolish search for power, Dahut opened the levies that protected Ys from the water that we had once reclaimed the land from, and all at once the former grand civilization of Ys and most of its people were drowned. And from the depths of the water, as you can see on this page, came the horrid Devil and instantly he and God began to fight. One fought for the salvation of His people and the other for his own selfish desires of conquest."

"The dragon won?"

"Mostly, you pick up rather quickly. Both were wounded in the bout, yet God received the worst of it. He retreated from battle into the depths of the tower until His strength recovers. The Devil flew off across the land, cursing it beneath him, cutting us off from the rest of mankind. There weren't many who survived the flood and made it to the tower in time. But those who did, he left them bewitched in Dahut's favor thus fulfilling his promise to her. And made it impossible for us to speak of her guilt. Ever since then, she's led them down a path of immorality. She awaits the day Satan returns and claims Ys for his own."

"You weren't bewitched? No curse has been placed on you?"

"No, my possession of this book, with its holy powers, kept me and only me free from both spells. The first being an inclination to be loyal to Dahut and the second being the spell of silence. Those devoted to the church, such as myself, my daughter, and a few select others, were protected from the bewitching curse that would make us slaves to her. Although they weren't saved from the spell of silence, as they did not have as much protection from the evil as me.

Yet my advanced age has weakened my mind and made me susceptible to her magical influence. As it goes, the tower was left unfinished and now God exists wounded beneath, while Dahut uses her influence to feed the barrier that surrounds Him to keep Him dormant."

"And how does she do that?"

"The brainwashed people... They believe the dragon is God now, and to keep the Devil at bay, they must..."

"Make a sacrifice. I know. I've seen it."

"The first born."

"I don't understand. If this is true, why don't you just have her killed? Do it yourself if the guards wont?"

"I'm too weak to lift a sword and I don't have it in me to kill my own daughter," the king put down the book and walked over to his bed, slowly sitting on it. "Besides, even if she dies, it would make no difference. The people believe what they believe. They are not the root of the problem."

"But why me? What do I have to do with it?"

"The magic of the cursed forest doesn't seem to affect you. I believe with what little power God has left, He created you to help us – to free us from the curse that surrounds Ys and to free Him as well. That's why I need you to do something for me, for all of Ys..." Ru gulped and clenched his fists. "I need you to travel through the cursed Dracon Lands, find the Devil himself and slay him for us. For all of humanity. So long as he exists in this plane of existence, no civilization is free from his destruction. Surely, all mankind will falter."

A great pressure suddenly weighed on Ru's shoulders. He breathed deeply and walked back a few steps. He wasn't sure if he could do what was being asked of him. But he remembered the innocent children of Ys that wandered its streets, and his friends Peter and Dana and concluded, "I'll do it!" he loudly declared.

Dana came bursting through the door with a speed in her step. "Wait!" She shouted. "I'm going with him! Father, you know why I've been running away – to do the very same thing you just asked of him! To help Ys in some way. It wouldn't- "

"Yes." The king cut her off with a quick agreement. He stood up and repeated himself. "You can go, but how can I know for sure you'll be safe? While he's fighting the dragon, who will protect you?"

"I'll bring Julia."

"Your servant? Well, that is better, but…" The king put his fingers to his chin as if he was thinking hard. "I want somebody who is skilled with the sword to accompany you, as well. Ah! That's it, Marcel will join you. He's the most skilled in all of Ys and a great navigator. He'll be able to help direct you southeast, where the Dragon went and keep you in bountiful territory, so you won't go hungry."

Ru interrupted, "Who is Marcel?"

"You've seen him," Dana answered, "my sisters royal guard. Father, I question if Dahut will allow that."

"I'll write a decree down and have it delivered to him," Mordred replied. "Let me do it now." The king returned to his desk and wrote on parchment with ink and then handed it to Dana. "Give this to the guard on your way out, dear. It has my seal on it." Mordred held his daughters' hands and looked at her with his pale, placid eyes, "I love you, my dear daughter. Do be safe. Ru, keep her safe, promise me."

Ru looked at Dana's innocent, green eyes, as wide as they were, filled with earnestness and vitality, he couldn't deny the old man his wish. "Always."

The two said their goodbyes as they left the King's room and exited to the hallway where they met the guards. Dana ordered them to give the decree to Marcel. She then retrieved Julia, and the three went down the elevator once more to the base. Julia walked ahead of the two, gathered some provisions at the market, and then headed to the exit of Ys as Ru and Dana took their time walking together.

"So, you were listening the entire time?" Ru asked Dana.

"Yes."

"I'm glad you could hear the truth straight from the source. Now I understand Dana, now I get it! Why you ran away and what's wrong with the city. The bells below were ringing for me to come here, so we can defeat the Devil together." Dana didn't reply. She grabbed his shirt with teary eyes. It seemed as if she wanted to speak but the curse wasn't allowing her. "Don't worry, Dana," Ru put his arms around her, hugging her gently, consoling her. Her arms loosely wrapped around him as she wept. "I see. Finally, I see. You're no longer alone." Holding her, any sense of doubt and pressure he felt before was gone.

Marcel kneeled before Dahut, staring at her exposed body, with parchment in hand. She was sprawled out on the fainting couch relishing in pleasure. The room was filled with others in a similar fashion and the air reeked of it. Only Marcel was not allowed to participate, yet he only had eyes for one and she seemed to take great joy in teasing him.

"My Princess," Marcel spoke, fixated on the scene in front of him. "I've received the order, like you planned."

Dahut spoke with a flushed face, "I see. Aren't I a genius? He told me what He wanted but it is my cunning implementation that will make it work. Ru and the others will go to the dragon, fight it and after killing it," She stopped as the head between her legs came up for air. She shoved him back in. "Ah, after killing it Ru will be weak, and then you will kill them. Once you do this for me, my little Marcel, you can finally have what you desire." She caressed her breasts and smiled at him, teasing him.

He gulped and grew pale, as tense as ever, his eyes widened at the thought. Teeth clenched and sweating profusely – he was ready. Ready for her. "How will I return without him? I cannot travel through the cursed lands alone."

Dahut snapped her fingers and a man came from across the room and fed her grapes straight from the vine. "Don't you see, my little Marcel? Once they kill the dragon, there will be no Dracon Lands and no mermaids. We will be free. Your only worry should be about getting lost. The world is everchanging, even the most accurate of…maps might not do any good. That is not something we can help you with. He can't control His effects on the Earth yet."

"Hm, I'll try my best. How can you guarantee that the boy can kill the dragon? A wyvern is one thing… But the dragon is several times its size. Not to forget its divine powers…"

"Don't doubt me. Ru is the only one who could kill it. After all, they are of the same ilk. I saw the proof with my own eyes. Now, don't you have someplace to be?"

Marcel took one final look at her body as it writhed in carnal joy and left. A wide crooked smile littered his grim face.

"I didn't expect you back so soon, lad."

Ru entered Peter's house, "why not? You're one of the few friends I have."

Peter looked at him with a hooked eyebrow and a following laugh, "well that's very kind of you. How can I help?"

"It's more of a matter of what I can do for you."

"Eh…what do you mean?"

"The king has sent us, Dana and I, on a journey to kill the dragon. We're allowed to bring others as well. Julia is also coming. I figured you'd like to come, maybe along the way you'll find what you're missing – your memories. Considering when they were taken from you, I think once I kill the dragon those memories will return."

"But-"

"Don't worry," Ru noticed the wanting in Peters eyes, "we know the truth. The king told us."

"And…Dana knows of this as well?"

"Yes, of course."

Peter paused for a moment; his eyes looked about as if searching for something. "All right. If Dana is going, then I'll go as well." Peter turned around and entered what appeared to be a storage space. While rummaging through, he made some noises that could only come from metallic objects. He shouted from afar, "I assume you have a plan then!?"

"For what?"

"Self-defense!" Peter returned brandishing a sheathed broadsword and handed it to Ru. "I'm sure there are plenty of monsters out there. We'll be needing some weapons. Go ahead, open her up."

Ru did so and found a slick, golden blade with a reflective sheen. However, the bottom of the blade was the color of a typical steel sword, it looked as if the sword had been mended together with a new blade. It was a two-handed sword, yet his superior strength allowed him to swing it about nimbly with one. It sang in the air as Ru slashed the air, practicing with the sword.

"What's the story with this weapon? I can feel there is something more to it. And why the difference in color?" Ru was quite curious.

"That sword belonged to Dana's grandfather, King Arthur. He pulled it from a stone which proved his right to rule. It broke in battle and his son, Mordred, inherited it once he died."

"So, how did you get it?"

"Before my time in the church, I worked in the armory for the military, since I'm so keen with metalwork. What was left of that sword we used as a basis to make new weapons, since it was so powerful. But as the years went by, and Ys became cut off because of the forest, there was no need for much of a military or new weapons. Nobody cared about the past anymore, or what it stood for. Not even the king. So, one day I just took it for posterity reasons, and no one was the wiser. I wanted to make sure that it was given to Dana and not her sister. I reworked it the best I could, but I figure you can wield it better than she would. It was meant to be used to protect her. Enough dawdling, are you satisfied? Now, tie it to your waist."

Ru put the magnificent weapon back in its brown sheath and followed Peters instruction. Ru noticed the older man had equipped himself with a more medium sized sword. "Then, let us be off," Ru proclaimed.

Before leaving and locking up his house, Peter ordered him to get a wooden cart and help him fill it with armor that he made over the years; for their other companions. Ru put on his lightweight steel armor first, only just on his shoulders, torso, forearms, and legs. The two left the house and walked through the fields.

"My only regret," Peter said as he looked longingly at his home, "is that no one will watch after the fields once I've gone!"

Ru chuckled, "don't worry, I'm sure the animals will tend to them dearly and fertilize them regularly." The two shared a laugh as they came upon the road and joined the others at the gate that opened to the wilds beyond Ys.

Dana quickly approached her old friend Peter and the two rejoiced in sharing each other's company once more. Julia joined them as well and the three were happy to be reunited after years of not being allowed to see each other. Peter convinced Dana of applying more armor, yet Julia didn't feel comfortable wearing it at all and put it aside. Just as it seemed the four were ready to leave, a voice called to them from behind. Ru turned to meet it.

"Don't forget about me. I've received my orders and I intend to fulfill them." Marcel had approached them from behind and despite being fully armored, except for a helmet, he was eerily light footed. He rested one hand on his waist above his sword and the other he held a large piece of parchment. "You won't get far without me, princess, despite how strong your guard supposedly is. Not without a map."

Peter snapped and approached Dahut's royal guard, "what the hell are you doing here? I thought it was just the four of us!?"

"No," Dana reproached, "father said we needed another sword with us. It was the only way he'd allow it."

"'The best in all of Ys'," Marcel said with a smile, "and don't you forget it, old man. With me and this map, we'll surely have no problems getting to the dragon."

"A map?" Ru replied, "this is the first I'm hearing of this."

Julia interrupted, "A map over a decade old would be of no use to us, after the…event. Not after the cursed forest sprang up. Who knows what else changed about the geography since."

"Don't worry that pretty little head of yours, handmaiden. And don't forget your position compared to mine. Even if the entirety of the land has changed, the stars remain the same. And there was no one better than me at roaming the kingdom of Ys without getting lost back in the day."

"And you, little knight," Dana replied, "don't forget your position compared to mine – and your duty to protect me from any dangers."

"Oh, I haven't, princess. I haven't. But how, may I ask, do you plan on all of us getting through that forest without burning alive?"

"I've already solved that problem," Ru answered.

The lot followed him down the road, through the threshold of the gate and onto the bright boarders of the roasted, cursed forest. Ru entered the land alone and searched for several minutes, until he returned with a gigantic companion. Dana stood steadfast but the others fell back in fear as he approached pulling the wyvern along.

"It's missing an eye," Marcel commented.

"It's the one we tamed yesterday," replied Ru. "I tied it up, but it managed to get loose. Possibly because it turns into spirit at night. Luckily it hadn't moved much from where we left it. No need to be frightened, as long as I am with it, it won't hurt you. It's under my command." The creature, with what seemed to be great reluctance, crossed the threshold between the forest and Ys' territory. "It can't exist long outside the cursed forest. Don't worry, so as long as I'm touching it, and you all are touching it as well, the curse of the land won't affect you either. My ability will extend unto you."

"And how do you know this?" Marcel questioned.

Dana, with great confidence in her voice, said, "he just does."

"Whatever. We should get going now, don't want to waste the sunlight."

"But where are we going?" Julia asked the party. A question that they all seemed to agree needed answering. "We're supposed to get to the dragon, but we don't know where it is. The last time anybody from Ys saw it, he flew over this direction. But he could've flown anywhere afterwards. Ys is but a small nation on a very large continent."

"True," Peter agreed, "We've acted hastily and foolishly. We've begun a journey without a plan. A beginning and end with no middle."

"Look at this," Marcel pulled out his map and laid it on the ground so all could see. "This is what the land around Ys looked like.

Ys exists on the western shore, the cliffside of a region called Brittany. To the southeast is where the dragon flew after it's fight with God. With some luck, hopefully we will find clues on our journey. We have no other choice."

"Yet this isn't a map of the entire continent, just of Brittany," Peter countered. "What if he flew farther than the map shows?"

Dana added her piece, "then perhaps I'll just have to ask other nations for help. Certainly, they must have seen the Dragon fly through the skies. As a princess, I am qualified to engage in such diplomatic discussions."

"Perhaps we should try to find other people?" Julia begged yet another question.

"Traveling to another country would be difficult, considering the distance," Marcel replied. "But it can be done. Just not so easily with an old man and two women. The closest is Loire. Perhaps, maybe, Ru has an idea?"

"I think it's a sound plan. If we take care of each other I think we can all make the trip. Now, let's get on the wyvern, he's growing impatient."

Dana, Peter, and Julia rode atop the scaled terror and as it lifted off it picked up Ru and Marcel with its large, clawed feet. Although they flew low, they flew strong, and they all shared in the amazement of flight as they traveled across the sun-burnt forest, hoping to reach the other side before the stormy night.

CHAPTER FIVE

The wyvern landed with such apparent exhaustion that it nearly tripped over itself once it met the ground. Ru found himself separated from the party as just moments prior the creature's weak grip dropped him and Marcel onto the patchy grass. He had no fear of the party being in trouble, however, for the forest was well behind them and the curse no longer a threat. But as he approached and looked upon the group as they steadied themselves from the sudden landing, the once virile wyvern laid itself down. It seemed to be suffering from the effects of carrying five people over several miles, its wings coiled around its torso as it trembled and whined. The thing closed its eyes to rest.

The party regrouped and, all except Marcel, rejoiced at how amazing it was to fly and complemented Ru on his ability to tame the beast and nullify the effect of the cursed forest. Ru could feel the warmth of his cheeks as he blushed at each compliment. Julia and Peter looked up at him in what he thought was wonderment, yet he felt the way Dana looked at him seemed to be more akin to admiration. "It was nothing, truly," Ru replied. "Everyone has their talents."

"I'm a good armorer," Peter responded, "but I can't tame a beast like that."

"I'm well versed in first-aid but that's nothing compared to counteracting the curse!" Julia exclaimed.

"He *is* quite amazing," Dana stated.

Ru found it all to be embarrassing but before he could deflect, he heard a loud thwomping sound coming from behind Peter and the women. A sorrowful cry commanded his attention like nothing before. He jolted through the group to find Marcel piercing the wyvern's neck with his broadsword, slowly killing it with each inefficient thrust. The thickness of the monster's scales made it difficult for the sword to pierce it, yet Marcel continued with haste, until the beast gushed with blood and was decapitated. The black-haired knight turned around, blood dripping from his face, as he smiled at the group. He spoke, "so it won't kill us in our sleep. You're welcome."

All celebration ended as the four looked at the face of the dead wyvern, now separated from its twitching body. Its visage lifeless, eyes vacant, Julia fell to the ground and cried while Dana buried her face in Ru's chest.

"What the bloody hell was that for!?" Peter shouted.

"What? What's your problem!?" Marcel said. "I saved you all. Instead of crying you should be thanking me. Praise me! Not him. He can tame it, but I can kill it."

"Curse you!" Ru shouted. "It was never going to hurt us, look at the sky!" The party looked up at the skies deep-evening glow. "The wyverns have a cyclical life cycle. Their lifespans are much faster than ours. During the hours of the day, they roam the forest in physical form. In the morning they are children and by evening, elderly. At night, they die, and their souls roam the forest searching for hosts to inhabit until morning comes again when they are reborn. This wyvern…was already near death. It gave the last of its life to fly us across the forest. But you killed it prematurely."

"So what?"

"Which means you removed it from its cycle of birth, death, and resurrection. Who knows what will happen to its soul…"

"Who cares about some damn lizard anyways!?"

"It was harmless!" Peter cried out. "Don't you see? Of course, you wouldn't."

"Damn you all." Marcel began to walk away as he spoke his final piece, "I'm making camp over here."

The four saw him off with disdain but decided, that due to the time of day, it was probably best to also make camp (but in a separate place) to rest for the journey ahead. Ru and Dana went together into the nearest patch of woods and looked around for the most suitable shrubbery to use for a fire. The shade from the trees above warranted them to stay close. While the two looked about, Ru noticed Dana's slow pace and overall lackadaisical demeanor. He approached her with open arms. She hugged him and, bursting at the seams with tears, she began to sob.

"You've never seen death before have you?" Ru whispered. The silence of the dense forest made the moment feel private. And her warmth, tenderness, and fragility everlasting.

Dana responded in between sniffles as she rubbed her eyes, "not since I was a child. I know it's ridiculous, just yesterday the thing would've killed me without a second thought." She paused, swallowed, and then continued, "but the look on its face – it looked so sad, so tired. So much…pain. It helped me fly… And now, suddenly, it's gone. He killed it Ru! All that blood…"

Ru tightened his embrace and drew closer to Dana, his face coming down to hers. "Won't you stop crying? How can I make these tears stop?"

"I can't – I can't…"

Ru put his lips to Dana's, her eyes growing wide. He didn't know what he was doing, he was just following his instincts – his heart. Ru simply wanted her to feel better and this was his only recourse. He feared she would run away, but quickly she responded with a kiss of her own. The silence of the dark forest was outmatched by the magic of their lips and any thought of the wyvern had, at least in that moment, passed.

The two stopped as things came to a breaking point – both noticed physical reactions and desires that had never been explored were beginning to arise. They looked into each other's eyes deeply, breathing heavily. Neither spoke. Which would win, the heart or the mind?

Julia called out to Dana from outside the forest, asking if the two needed any help gathering wood. Quickly, they stood apart.

"I should go," Dana said.

"Right. Be there soon."

Dana picked up some sticks and branches and hurried off to the clearing where they landed. Ru stood alone in the forest and quickly sat down at the base of a tree collecting himself. *'What am I doing? What came over me? I've never felt that way before. But her eyes were so beautiful, even though she was crying. Her lips so full. Her body supple, yet… ample. What is this?'* A strange feeling of guilt crawled over him. He picked up some wood and returned to the fire, where Dana, surrounded by an unknowing Julia and Peter, continued to look up at him with bashful doting eyes.

He didn't mind this at all.

A haze of smoke and fire morphed into a figure all too familiar and yet so foreign. Gigantic wings, four legs, and a long deadly tail. From the blurry figure he heard a vicious cry – a sound like that of a wyvern but much more terrifying. The cry, while not in the common language, was something he understood well.

Ru awoke in a cold sweat and confused craze. The cerebral nightmare left such an impact on him that it took several calls of concern from his friends to calm him down. It was Dana's voice that truly eased his nerves.

"Ru! Ru! Are you alright? It was just a dream, calm down," Dana called out to him, so concerned that she hugged him closely. Ru could see the surprise in Julia's eyes at the fact, and so, he politely pulled her away.

"I'm fine everyone, really," Ru said to calm everyone.

"That must've been your first nightmare," Peter said. "Am I wrong?"

"A nightmare? I suppose so, but maybe not."

"Are you lot done coddling him?" Marcel approached from afar. After a night to himself, the groups attitude towards him still hadn't softened. "Did the tough guy have a bit of a fright?" He laughed as the group scowled his way.

"I'm fine." Ru stood up with Dana's help, in a bit of a daze.

"Finally. We should get going now—"

"Wait," Ru interrupted Marcel. "Can you show me your map once more?" Marcel reluctantly complied and Ru looked studiously at the map for several minutes.

"Well, Ru," Dana said, "What is it? What about the map? Are you all right?"

Ru finally answered, "Yes, sorry. If Ys was truly the center point of the dragon's fixation, then I doubt it would stray far from the country. Marcel, what can you tell me about this point here, the part on the edge with dotted lines?"

"That's the Silver Shore. The only part of Loire with a significant coastline. It used to belong to Ys, once we took it, but since we got cut off from the rest of the world, they've surely reclaimed it by now. It's this area's best natural port, especially since, like I said before, most of Brittany's shorelines are cliffs and not suited for boats."

"Silver Shore…" Ru spoke to himself, remembering the dream he had just moments before. "That's where we need to go, southeast, to there."

"What makes you say that?"

"My dream just now, I dreamt of a dragon and it cried out to me one single phrase: 'To the Silver Shore.'"

The band stood aghast, surprised at such a fortunate turn of events. Dana was the first to reply, "Yes! I knew it all along! I knew that if I left Ys, I would find help."

"No Dana," Ru replied, "there can be no help from the Devil. I believe it was more like a call to challenge. He knows we're coming to slay him. It stands to reason he would rather have the fight sooner rather than later. It's an attempt at intimidation." Dana looked worrisome at Julia and Peter, and they responded in a similar fashion. "Don't worry everyone, I'll not lose the battle."

"Strange though, isn't it?" Marcel spoke with a wry smile. "How the Devil seems to speak to you and you alone?"

"What are you trying to say?"

"Nothing, nothing at all. Here let me plot this…" Marcel took a few moments but after thinking, he used a small pencil to mark the map. "This would be the safest way to the Silver Shore. I suppose we're at this point already, if I calculated the distance we've crossed so far correctly."

"How can you be so sure?"

"Years ago, I was naught but a simple soldier roaming the countryside with my troop. I learned the land of Ys well, all the roads and landmarks…its geography, like the back of my hand."

"Then I'll leave it to you. Lead the way."

Marcel continued ahead into the lush forest as the group followed behind along the dirt road. Peter counted his blessings – the fact they had come so far could only be a sign from God Himself. This was his only opportunity to set things right and make up for his failure ten years ago. He looked at Marcel and grew anxious. Peter grabbed Ru's ear and spoke to him secretly, "I don't like this. I don't trust him. Lad, if you have any wit about you, you'd kill him now and take the map for yourself."

"I don't like him much either, Peter. But he's done nothing so far to warrant death."

"I've known this man for years. I know his character. He killed the wyvern – it was helpless and defenseless. It may have been a beast, but even dogs were once beasts until they were tamed. If he's capable of that, then he's capable of anything. Do it now while his back is turned, or mark my words, there will come a time where he will smite you."

Dana and Julia turned to the two and listened avidly for Ru's response. "I can't do that," Ru replied. "To kill for what someone might do and not for what they have done, is just as he did; an evil thing. Peter, for suggesting it, can you say you are any better than he? Let's forget this discussion, my friend, and move on. There is a long journey ahead and I'd rather not begin it on a sour note."

Shame showered over Peter and the guilt of his suggestion overcame him. Julia came to his side to console him, "I'm…sorry. If it's any consolation, I was thinking the same thing you were. He is an evil man."

"No Julia, he was right. And I respect him even more for it. But I wonder, if he knew the truth, would he still think the same?"

CHAPTER SIX

Several days passed while Marcel led the group of heroes down a long and winding path, up through hills that drastically, almost unbelievably, dipped and rose at such extremes that they seemed like miniature mountains. The trees, too, seemed to have some strange affect to them. With every wind that blew, their limbs followed uniformly, as if having an amorphous property contrary to their sturdy appearance.

Recently, Marcel had become very short-tempered, especially at Peter who was very quick to criticize the royal guard. Ru could tell Marcel was trying to prove himself as a leader, yet everyone else in the group was beginning to vocalize doubt whether he knew where he was going. Tempers began to shorten since the group had run out of the provisions. When the next meal would come was a constant concern since wild animals and fresh water weren't as abundant as they once assumed.

Ru continued to notice the increasingly strange turn in nature the further into the wilderness they went. As they passed a field of wheat, he saw that the grassy ground had turned from an emerald green to a sapphiric blue. "This is strange, right?" Ru asked aloud to the others.

"It's as blue as my hair!" Dana exclaimed.

"Was it like this before, Marcel?"

Marcel took a moment to respond, but eventually murmured, "no."

"Of course, it wasn't!" Peter shouted. "You've been leading us on a wild goose chase this entire time. Let's face it, the whole region's been changed, not just the immediate land around Ys. Admit it!"

Marcel turned around with a vicious scowl and stepped aggressively toward Peter. Ru stood between the two, holding out the palms of his hands, saying, "stop, the both of you. Marcel, is it true? Are you lost?"

"It's not my fault!" He replied, begrudgingly answering the question. "Everything's changed – all the landmarks I remembered are gone. All the freshwater streams and usual hunting spots I remembered from years ago – it's all gone! Everything is crazy! The grass is blue!? Just an hour ago I stepped on a pebble, a small little thing. I should've tripped at worst but instead I bounced off it. Like it pushed me away, forcing me to jump off the ground almost. And that's not even the worse of it…"

"How could things be worse!?" Dana added. "We haven't come across any food in days and there is hardly any water. Poor Julia is starving. You all may not have noticed but she's been giving some of her portions to you two -"

Julia tried to interject, "please, Dana, don't -"

"No, Julia, Marcel needs to know. She's been handing out the food for everyone and has been giving a bit of her own for you and Ru."

"Why?" Ru asked Julia.

"I…wanted to make sure you all had the strength to lead and protect us."

Dana continued, "it's always been part of your charitable nature. You were a nun, after all. We were wrong to think there would be plentiful wildlife to eat."

"Nobody asked you to do that!" Marcel shouted at Julia. "Don't try to guilt me into owing you a favor."

"I never…" Julia amplified her already terrible condition with every attempt to reason her good intentions. "It's not fair…!" Dana caught her just as she lost her balance and nearly fell.

"Damn it!" Marcel continued. "Everything has gone wrong! I didn't want to say this… But the stars at night have changed as well."

"Which means?" asked Peter.

"It means that I can't even position us or give any direction at all! I would've been able to at least tell if we were going north or south, but the stars out here are not the same as in the city."

Ru could read the desperation on everyone's faces. He was rather hungry and becoming very tired. He could tell his stamina was far greater than his allies', so he could only figure their exhaustion must've been tenfold. He could see Julia had a far weaker constitution than the others. She was middle-aged and always seemed to be quite frail. If only he had been more proactive in keeping up with their provisions, then she wouldn't be suffering. His selfishness weighed on his conscience and he knew he had to make up for it.

"We'll solve the most immediate problem first. Food and water. Peter and Dana, you take Julia over there into the shade and rest. Look under logs for insects and mushrooms we can eat." Ru noticed Dana grimacing at the thought. "I don't like it either, but while Marcel and I go further into the woods in search of something more tasteful we need a backup plan. Does everyone understand?"

The group muttered in agreement and went on their way. Ru and Marcel went off the path they'd been following and delved further into the thickets, leaving the others to scavenge in the shade.

An hour had passed, and the two men had finally tracked down a doe and cornered it in a crevice next to a stone wall. It was a bizarre thing. The deer, much like the environment around it, had been changed. It had bulbous eyes and a coat as black as tar. Nothing about the creature seemed appetizing. The men hid in some bushes, stalking their prey.

"What the hell is wrong with it?" Marcel whispered.

"Even the animals have been affected by the curse. And look at that, what is it drinking?" Ru pointed out a small fountain of purple liquid, leaking down from the cliff above into a stream which the doe drank from.

"It's not water. And look at the grass around it – it's similarly purple. Hmph."

"We can do this together. I'll come from the left and you- "

"I don't think so! I've had enough of being outshined by you." Marcel jumped out of the bushes, unsheathed his sword, and rushed the deer with great speed. Yet, as soon as he stepped on the purple grass, he keeled over almost instantly. "What is this?" He faintly cried out. Ru figured the poisoned land must've had a sort of energy-draining ability.

He noticed just in the nick of time the stag, which was hiding in the forest, jolting towards Marcel to protect its mate. The male deer lowered its head, rushing to attack with its deadly antlers. Ru came out even faster and made it in just enough time to take the piercing blow for Marcel. Ru was lifted several feet in the air and jerked around by the mighty animal, blood from his stomach flowing down onto the ground below. He screamed in agony as the beast jerked its head about flinging him across the way, slamming him against the rock wall and sliding down into the purple puddle. The open wound bled profusely into the liquid.

Once Ru's blood varnished the purple grass, it returned to its normal, green color, and suddenly Marcel was able to move. The stag had turned its back to the knight, and he seized the opportunity. He took his sword and stabbed its stomach from below. It fell to the ground and jerked around. He finished it off, cutting off its head. Afterward, he turned to Ru and walked to him only to see the most amazing sight.

As Ru's blood diluted into the purple liquid, the clearer it became. Ultimately, the purple substance began to sparkle until no signs of any color at all tarnished it. It and the stream it came from, had become clear, fresh drinking water.

"What the hell!?" Marcel said in shock and awe.

Ru stepped out of the stream holding his lower abdomen and lifted his shirt to check on the wound. Shocking them both, there was no wound to find. What had once been a gaping, bleeding hole was now sealed over by thick, green scales.

"What are you?" asked Marcel.

"I-I don't know."

"The way you heal, and your blood, it cured the poisoned water and grass... What devilry is this?"

"Devilry? I'm no… I'm not a devil. I promise. I don't know why these things are happening."

"Eavesdropping, I had overheard the others talk about you. I thought it was just some campfire story about a man born from the Dracon Lands. Maybe you are a devil after all, it would explain how he spoke to you the other night. And, why the princess has been…"

"Been what?"

"Keeping you company at night."

Despite the shade, Dana and the others still suffered from the sweltering heat. For a little over an hour the three suffered; silently awaiting their companions' arrival. Unusually large gnats and mosquitos harassed the trio to no end, to the point where their nerves began to break. Peter lost his temper and began to go after just about every pest he could see, while Julia relaxed on a tree stump, too hungry to move, and Dana hunched over a log collecting any sort of insect she could find.

Dana's back began to grow stiff and ache, so, deciding she had done enough, sat down unknowingly close to Julia's head.

"I'm beat!" Dana exclaimed as she placed the pile of bugs she collected behind her.

"Gross…" Julia murmured.

"Are you complaining? I caught these for you. I don't want to eat them either, but we haven't a choice. I'm just too tired right now to continue."

"And what are you tired of?"

"What?"

"Lack of sleep?"

"No, why do you ask?"

Julia didn't respond and Dana's mind spurred wild until she realized what she meant. She stood up, greatly offended.

"How could you!? You know why I'm laying with him. He's been having nightmares every night since the dream of the dragon. Only my presence calms him."

"And why is that?"

"You wouldn't understand – he and I have a connection. I was the one who was there when he hatched – the first one he saw. I cleaned his mouth so he could breathe. I think that's why he's so relaxed with me."

"Are you his mother, or something more?"

Peter approached the two and asked if everything was alright. He was ignored.

"What is your problem?" Dana continued.

"I'm hungry and I don't want this…filth!" Julia shoved the worms and bugs away, scattering them across the ground. She began to weep.

"Hey!" Dana shouted.

"I didn't think it would be this hard! At least in Ys I never starved!"

Peter interrupted, "gather yourself, woman! Are you not a nun, a follower of God? Be thankful for the food He has provided. For what Dana has provided. Don't take your difficulties out on your friends, we have so very few already. Can't you see we are all hungry?"

Dana continued, still frazzled and fixated by what Julia had accused of her. "I've done nothing like that with him. And even if I did, even if I wanted to, didn't you say it would be normal?"

Julia responded, "normal to have such feelings. But sleeping with a man, sex or not, before marriage is wholly inappropriate, Dana. You know that."

Peter looked up at Dana and said, "I didn't want to say it, but when you started to lay with him, I also felt it to be suspect."

"Well, you know what!?" Dana shouted at Julia. "What good are you? I'm supporting him, our best chance, the best I can. What if the only one of us strong enough to fight off a monster just ups and faints during a battle due to exhaustion? Yet, all you can do is lay down and complain. Well, why don't you just do us all a favor, die already!" Dana turned around and hastily walked into the forest, eventually running. Running further in as fast as she could go, wiping the tears away from her face.

Dana instantly regretted what she said, but that was the only way she knew to offend Julia worse than she hurt her. She knew that Julia was helping Ru the best she could as well. She stopped running and eventually came to her knees next to a bush and continued to sob. 'I hate this! I hate her! I hate...me.' After collecting herself she stood and turned back to where she entered the forest. *'I ought to go apologize. She's almost like...my mother, after all.'* Yet as she walked back, she came across Ru and Marcel as they were also returning to the others.

"Are you okay?" Ru asked.

Dana noticed his concerned smile and the buck he carried across his shoulders. "I am now. Let's go."

Marcel smirked as he walked by and ahead of the two. Yet they didn't let it bother them. Eventually, Dana returned to the tree stump with Ru by her side and made eye contact with Julia, an action that probably didn't help the situation, since the two walked with a smile. Dana felt it best not to talk about it with her, at least for now. Not while he was around.

The fire was blazing, yet moods had soured to an unexpected low. The deer's physiology had been altered so that one bite caused a great pain in one's teeth. Pain so incredible, that the thing was practically inedible. Julia was the first to give up and sleep, and the others soon followed. Dana knew that the others were watching – judging – and she also knew that they were right, at least to some extent. While approaching him and lying with him to sleep, she knew she was doing it for more than what she claimed. There was a pleasure to it. To be with the man she liked, to be held in the arms of the only one that could protect her from this wide and scary world. To have him run his fingers through her silky, blue hair. But she also knew that it was wrong and every now and then, in the back of her mind, she began to remind herself of her sister.

Night passed as Dana slept comfortably dreaming of a sweet song while being held warmly in a white, clandestine space.

Peter awoke the party in a frantic craze. "I can't find her! Julia is gone!"

Dana jolted to her feet and with great concern asked, "What? Where is she? Where did she go?"

"I don't know! I woke up but ten minutes ago and noticed she was gone. I didn't want to alert anyone too soon, but I think something's happened."

"Where did you see her last?" Ru interjected.

"It was after everyone else had fallen asleep. I couldn't sleep well last night, so I stayed up late. I heard a strange noise coming from around the tree stump…it was her. She was picking the ground where she threw the bugs yesterday, desperately looking for something to eat. It…scared me, so I went away. I think she's gone mad!"

The three began to consider their options, whether to split up or not when searching for her and how far she could have gone. To go left, or right? What to do? Dana turned around to meet Marcel's call, "I swear you'd lot would be lost without me. Her tracks are right there, broken branches and footprints. She's headed towards where we came from yesterday, Ru. Where we found the water."

The four followed the path in search for their missing compatriot.

CHAPTER SEVEN

They followed Julia's tracks to where the men fought the stag the previous day. The four stood silently behind the trees and watched as the malformed doe from yesterday, the one that escaped, had returned to drink the now clear water. Marcel went for his sword, yet Ru stopped him. The group all watched in amazement while the deer drank the sparkling, clean water and saw that it returned to being a normal deer.

"The water cured it!" Peter whispered.

Marcel took this opportunity to charge the doe and kill it quickly. A short discussion occurred between the party whether to eat it now or continue searching for the woman, but ultimately their hunger persuaded them to return to camp and consume it. The action was rationalized by the thought that being starved themselves, they wouldn't be able to search properly for her. In addition, it was believed that if they had some food with them, they could ease her hunger pain once they arrived. Ru remained quiet at camp as Marcel spoke of how his blood changed the water and transformed the deer and that such strangeness must be an omen of things to come. Dana and Peter merely looked at each other and continued to eat.

After finishing the meal, they returned to the spot with the water once more and took a drink of the clear water. Marcel spit the liquid out claiming it was disgusting, while the others enjoyed its freshness as it had been quite some time since they'd last partaken. "How can you two drink that sewage water knowing his blood is in it?" Marcel questioned.

The others ignored him, thanked Ru, and continued on their way, following the trail Julia left behind. As the crew walked on, the more cautious they became. Eventually, the ground returned to its normal state, relatively flat with green grass and the trees stood strong and sturdy. They lost sight of any possible tracks and became lost in the lush forest. What was even more confusing was the sudden liveliness of the area – birds of every color tweeting out their favorite song while almost every animal Ru could think of roamed about carelessly, even in sight of predator or prey, strolling with their mate. Each animal was paired with another of the same species of the opposite sex. A calming sunshine filtered through the trees above as a cool breeze set in and distracted the party even more.

"Where are we?" Ru asked aloud. "Something isn't right… This peace isn't normal."

"Damn right," Marcel looked about with a cold sweat.

"I don't know," Dana said. "I really like it. There is so much life here. It's like the garden I had as a child. Look at that butterfly! And down there, watermelon!" Dana skipped ahead of the group into the entangled greens of the melons.

"Don't stray too far now, child!" Peter warned.

Ru sensed an immediate danger – the animals had become vacant and the wind stopped. "Dana, come ba-" Suddenly, she fell into the greens and was dragged away into the shadowy distance.

Peter screamed from behind, "Ru!"

Ru looked to see what Peter was pointing at – both of Peters feet had been wrapped by writhing vines. Vines so thick that no average man could break them. Quickly, Ru unsheathed his sword and prepared to set him free, yet as soon as he did, several vines shot up from the ground and wrapped themselves around his neck, arms, and thighs. He couldn't move. Only Marcel remained free. "Marcel!" Ru struggled to speak. "Cut us free!" Yet for some reason, which Ru couldn't deduce, he didn't; at least not at first. Marcel seemed to be scared stiff and when he did reach for his sword, Peter had already been dragged away in the same direction as Dana. Ru's face was turning blue and he could barely speak. He yelled, "hurry!" And when Marcel finally brought out his sword and began to swing it, he too was quickly jolted away by the vines, but in a different direction than the others.

Ru was alone – struggling. His great might had nearly torn the five vines apart, and when he finally snapped two, ten more sprang upon him, and ten more after that. He was out of air and strength. He drowned in them.

Ru awoke to the grunting and rustling of Peter. Dana, Peter, and himself had been tied to separate trees by the vines which had kidnapped them. To his immediate right was Dana and then to her right was Peter. Marcel was nowhere to be found. Ru attempted to break free from the vines and, after realizing he hadn't the strength, chewed through the one covering his mouth, allowing him to speak.

"Are you two all right?" He asked the others, who nodded yes in response. Ru examined his immediate surroundings, of which there were only two things of note: a simple log cabin to his front and to the right, surrounded by a field of dandelions and clovers, stood a large tree with the most delicious looking fruit growing from its branches. Red and shiny, they looked similar to apples. Before Ru could shout for help, the cabin door opened.

A nubile woman in a loose, translucent white dress came out barefoot. Her feet made almost no impression upon the blades of grass; it was as if she was the breeze itself. Aloof and avoiding eye contact, she slowly made her way to the tree. She plucked the fruit and then sat in the field, with her eyes finally meeting his own. He was stunned. Not at her beauty, no, but at her visage. The fleshy horns protruding from her forehead were the obvious points of distraction, but what followed was her unbelievably white hair, which countered her apparent youth. However, the closer Ru looked, the further he fell into the woman's gaze. He saw in her eyes a strangeness in her pupils, which leaked out into the outer edge of her blue iris'. They were akin to a drop of ink cascading down a canvas. She finally smiled and broke eye contact with him. The vines covering the mouths of the other two moved away as she did.

"I take it you're the one responsible for this?" asked Ru as he tried to get a read on the woman.

"This is sorcery!" Peter shouted. "Be careful, Ru, she isn't human!"

The horned woman, while plucking the clovers below, responded to Peter's claim, "I am human, I am not human. I am more, yet I am less."

"I don't care what you are," Dana said. "Where is Julia!?"

The woman smiled and as she did the door to the cabin opened once more and Julia, looking sicker than ever before, came out to meet her friends. She could only walk a few steps until she stumbled and fell to her knees.

"Julia! Are you okay? Has she hurt you?" Dana asked, obviously concerned.

Julia nodded and spoke faintly, "I'm…fine."

The horned woman interrupted, "this girl heard my song and in desperation came to me. I have not hurt her, in fact, I've done the opposite."

"What do you mean?" Dana asked.

"What song?" Ru added.

"I am so lonely in this garden. My brother left me and now all I have is my own voice to keep me company. This paradise, where your kind first fell, is all I have, and I can never leave. If I do, surely, I'll be killed. I do not think He has forgiven my kind; I also don't think He cares much for you, either. For how else would I be able to hide in such an obvious place? Since the realms merged, I, one of the last of my kind, found refuge here. This realm travels the Earth and I along with it. I sing a song that calls to those in search for salvation and they come to me."

"For what price?" Peter asked.

The woman smirked once more and continued on as if Peter's question was rhetorical, "she entered this realm willingly and I invited her into my cabin. Since it's made of the branches of this tree, while inside she felt no pain. But as you can see, once she leaves it, her pain and hunger has struck her all at once." Julia began to crawl back over the stone-laden ground towards the cabin; but as she did, the horned woman waved her hand and a thin vine wrapped itself around her ankle and kept her in place. "I'm sorry, my little one, but I am not done."

"Let her go! Let us all go!" Ru demanded. "We've done nothing to you. Why do you hold us hostage?"

"My distant cousins, there is nothing I hate more than you. Well, perhaps only your creator. You humans have been chosen by God. Favored. And there is a Grace in you that comes from that. Especially you four." The woman ceased to pluck the weeds and looked Ru in the eyes. "I am a nephilim, the daughter of an angel and human woman. My name is Ishla."

"I-impossible!" Peter shouted.

"I don't understand, what does that mean, Peter?" Ru asked, very confused at what Ishla meant.

"Ru…they taught us in church, the nephilim are the offspring of fallen angels – angels that defied God and attempted to usurp him long ago, before modern civilization. They were evil and brought misfortune to mankind. God flooded the Earth to rid it of them and sentenced the angels to Hell. He only saved the humans and animals. How could they have survived!?"

Ishla added, "we survived. It wasn't easy, but through the grace of Satan we found a way. Through him we found life. And it's only through his mercy and virtue that we thrive to this day. He never abandoned us. Not like yours has abandoned you."

"God hasn't abandoned us!" Ru interjected. "He's simply resting in Ys, healing until he can return. It's the Devil, your savior, that's holding him back."

"What?" Ishla smiled as if amused. "Oh, aren't you rather confused. I can see it now, it clouds the others but not you." She laughed aloud. "Yes, yes, you are right. Let's see, how about we play a little game, shall we?"

"I will play nothing. Release us! Or else, when I get free…"

"You will never know freedom as you are now. I can see there is something special about you, but you have not yet reached your full potential. My eyes can see things yours cannot yet see. Let's make a deal, if you can resist this fruit here in my hand, then I will let you go. But if you cannot, then you will be cursed to stay with me for all eternity. What do you say?"

Ru looked at the apple in her hand and as delicious as it seemed, there was something peculiar about it, something to him that seemed forbidden. It reminded him of the hole inside the tower of Ys. "No. That's a cursed fruit – your eyes are not the only ones that can see the unseen. It will damn whoever dares eat it."

"Well, do you or do you not have faith in your friends? Surely you must, and of course, you trust them enough to deny the fruit then? So, you have nothing to lose, really, if you play my lonely little game. All I ask is for some entertainment before you go. Or do you not believe in them? Do you not have faith in their ability to resist the temptation?"

Ru could feel the eyes of Peter, Dana, and Julia upon him. And after a short pause, he softly answered, "of course, I do."

Ishla stood up with glee and skipped over to Peter first. "Then let us play. You, old man, I can read you like a book. I can see your deepest desire. This fruit has the ability to give you the knowledge on how to gain what you want the most. All you must do is simply take one little bite and you will have the knowledge you seek – you will know how to create the carillon of Ys, its famous bells of yore. You will be free of your guilt."

Peter looked at the fruit, eyes wide and mouth salivating. He then looked at Ru and then to the fruit. He closed his eyes and turned his head away from the nephilim in rejection.

"I take that as a no?" Ishla giggled as she walked to her right, onto Dana next. "What a pretty princess. You heard what I said before. The knowledge you seek is all here. You're searching for…the dragon? Yet you haven't a clue as to how to get to the Silver Shore. It's all here, my dear. A small little bite wouldn't hurt, would it? Damnation is a small price to pay for the benefit of your entire civilization. It's rather selfish, actually, to not eat it; it's your purpose, after all, as princess, to save the people of your kingdom. No matter the cost."

"Never!" Dana instantly replied. "I was warned as a child by priests in the church of swindlers and soothsayers. Nothing good comes from the easy way out and fortune only befalls those willing to walk the road least traveled. I have the utmost faith that Ru is telling the truth about the fruit. While even I can't deny the fruits beauty, all I must do is look at how ugly the one offering it to me is and I know the truth. Now, leave me, demon!"

Ishla covered her eyes as if blinded by the sun as a faint white light flashed from Dana's body. Ru didn't quite understand what had just happened and by judging at Peter's (and Dana's) reactions, this was not something that had happened before. Ru was amazed at Dana, however, regardless of this mysterious event. Her resolve and morality made him admire her even more. Ishla composed herself and then walked to Ru next, giving up on her tempting of Dana. The smile that had left her face just moments before returned as she held out the fruit to him.

"Your turn," Ishla said.

"You know the answer," Ru replied defiantly.

"But you don't know the offer. Would you like to know how to find the Dragon? Or would you, perhaps, rather know who you really are? Or maybe…" From the corner of Ru's eye, he could see something above Dana – a snake slithering down the tree; its fangs exposed, it slowly reached her neck without her knowing. Ishla continued, "would you like to know how to make her love you as much as you love her?"

Dana gasped audibly and Peter was shocked as well. While Ru was also astonished, he was too concerned about the snake growing ever closer to Dana's neck. Ishla continued, "all you have to do is take a bite and everything will be *okay*." Ru could tell by how she spoke, how she looked at him, that she knew of the snake and that it was her doing. If he didn't take the apple, Dana would die, yet if he did, not only would he be damned, the journey to defeat the Devil would end in failure, as well. He couldn't make up his mind – his eyes switched from the apple to the snake and then to Dana several times, until chilling droplets of sweat fell down his brow. Fear engulfed him, and quickly the apple's red skin became so much more than tempting; it became his everything. Yet before he could decide or act a voice came calling from his left.

"Wait!" Julia called out weakly. "Will it give me what I want?"

"Hm?" Ishla said. "You? Leave me alone, woman."

Quickly and desperately, with the last of her strength, Julia jumped up at the nephilim, knocking her to the ground and stole the fruit from her hand. Julia had seemingly cut herself free from the vine which tied her down. She swiftly held the apple to her mouth just before she was interrupted.

"Wait!" Peter shouted. "Don't do it! Julia, we brought food with us. Ru has it! Ru, give -"

The crunch of the bite reverberated throughout the dense halls of the forest as all the world focused on her. Julia, who once walked in providence now had fallen to her knees, her hair turned white and her movements slick and provocative. Ishla laughed as she lay in the mire of clovers and dandelions. The vines holding the three to the trees left and the snake approaching Dana's neck retreated.

After hitting ground, Ru watched as Julia crawled over to the nephilim and nuzzled into her lap, caressing her breasts and kissing her from below. The snake from the tree slithered over, coiled around them, and joined in kind. Ru could see no grace left within Julia. With tears coming from his eyes, he unsheathed his sword and rushed towards the three with full intent to kill them. Dana jumped between him and his target and spoke without looking him in the eyes, "please…don't. She was like a mother to me. If this is what she wanted, then… I never got to say sorry. Please, for me…"

Ru couldn't breathe, he shook until his arm seemed to lower on its own. He turned from them and began to walk away. His need for justice left unfulfilled.

Peter hadn't calmed yet, he continued, "Is that it!? Ru, you're just going to let this be!? Kill the beast! Save her!"

"It would make no difference," replied Ru. "It's too late."

"Indeed," Ishla added. "Your kind is so beautiful when you're fallen."

"What the bloody hell was it all for!?" Peter continued, crying, "Julia! Can't you hear me? I've known you for years! Come back to me… What is it that you could have possibly wanted, more than, than…"

"Can't you see?" Ishla answered. "The Julia you once knew is no more. What she really wanted, in the end, was to be free from all mortal pains – all that bound her to suffering. Her morality. Now she is mine, and now I am not alone. I hope you can see now, Ru. Just how weak humans are. You may leave."

"Wait," Julia ceased her sin for one moment to speak to Dana, who too was crying at the sight. "Dana, my lovely, beautiful girl. I am so sorry about before, when we fought. I was wrong. I at least wanted you to know that before you left."

"No! No!" Dana responded. "You were right, Julia, mother, you were right. I won't do *it*. I won't."

"No, my dear, Ru is an attractive man. You should have sex with him, in fact. It will feel good, I promise."

"What!? No, you said all of that isn't appropriate."

"But don't you know, dear, sometimes something improper…is the most appropriate thing to do." Julia then went back to the nephilim and snake and returned to sin.

Ru continued to walk away into the forest followed by Dana and Peter. "Don't worry," he said aloud as they traveled blindly through the shrubbery; as the grass returned to its former color of blue, "God will punish them for this. One day, I'm sure."

The three walked in silence as more time passed. Peter silently sobbed until he could cry no more. Ru noticed Dana was oddly quiet and kept a great deal of distance from him. He could tell, now that the truth was out in the open, of how they felt about each other, their relationship had changed. He was sure it was for the worse. Of the decisions he'd made that day he thought to himself, *'Never again. Never again will I dance with fire.'*

The trees cleared and the three came to a dirt road where they found Marcel relaxing in some shade. "Ah, there you are. Took you long enough. Wait – where's the other one? The woman?" The knight asked.

Ru spent a short time explaining the basics of the situation and found that Marcel didn't know why he was taken away to a separate place. He claimed it made more sense to wait for the party to arrive and conserve energy rather than searching through the forest. Ru gave the explanation little thought and followed him in solemn silence.

CHAPTER EIGHT

Making camp was interrupted by the howl's and barking from the wolves which chased the four throughout the night. Dana unsheathed her small blade and slashed at one of the animals as it closed in to bite her. The beast dodged and instead clenched its jaws down on her sword and pulled it away. Ru came in from the front and sliced the wolf's head clean off as the party continued to run. She didn't thank him.

The wolves were not ordinary, a lot like the deer the party faced before, these creatures had similarly been altered; now standing five feet tall with blood-red eyes. They were ten times as fast and ferocious as normal wolves and, because of this, the group was struggling to keep them at bay. As they ran through the starry night across an open field, they were looking for some sort of natural shelter to hide in. It was Marcel who shouted, "there!" as he pointed towards a run-down building surrounded by a fence made of stones. The buildings' windows, Dana noticed as she deftly evaded another of the wolf's lunges, was flickering with light like that of a candle. The group quickly made their way down the hill as they fought off the animals, until they reached the flimsy, wooden door, barged in and shut it behind them. They looked out the windows to see if the wolves would follow, but the beasts simply surrounded the building instead, as if they were unable to follow them any further. Instead of leaving for other prey, it seemed the four-legged fiends were waiting for the group to eventually leave the building.

Just as the party began to calm, the screaming behind them caused them to nearly jump out of their skin. Dana gasped as she turned around, fearing that she had just left one danger only to find another. She was surprised at what she came to see. A young boy was calming two adults, who she assumed to be his parents, as they scuttled away in fear of the four intruders.

"It's okay, momma, papa! Do not worry! They will not hurt us – they cannot! Not here. Calm. Good, good." The boy patted his parents as if they themselves were dogs. They calmed after a short bit. The man and woman were short and stout, they walked on almost all fours, dragging their knuckles across the ground. The two were extremely hairy and muscular, more so than any other in the room. Their protruding brows hovered over their small eyes that skittered across the group.

"What in the world is wrong with them?" Marcel questioned.

Dana walked over to the boy with a smile. She kneeled down, getting to his eye level and asked kindly, "hello, my name is Dana. Sorry we came uninvited into your home, but we were attacked by wolves. This here is Peter and Ru. What is your name?"

The boy didn't leave his cowering parents' side, but he did reply, "Arland is my name. I am so glad to meet you! It's been a long time since I've seen somebody else. I've…been so alone."

She could feel Arland's burden and replied, "it's okay, dear, come here." Dana held out her arms and the boy embraced her with tears.

"Will somebody tell me what's going on?" Marcel asked.

Peter answered for Dana as she was comforting the lonely child, "It seems they're also hiding from the wolves."

"But look at his parents," Ru added. "They don't look normal."

Dana gave Ru a piercing gaze which caused him to turn away.

"It's okay. You are right, sir," Arland said. "My parents, like the rest of my people, have all turned into this. I'm the only one who remained normal."

"They look like…human apes?" Marcel stated.

"Quiet!" Dana said. "Don't be rude!"

"No, everyone please calm down and sit. There is no need to worry – those animals cannot hurt us. Nothing can hurt us in this safe haven." The boy began to move some wooden benches into a circle and beckoned everyone to sit. They all gathered around and sat between a weak, flickering candle. All except for Ru, who stayed in earshot, looking out the window at the beasts at bay.

"What did you mean, Arland, when you said nothing can hurt us here?" Dana asked as the group settled.

"This is a church of God... Me and my parents come from Nantes. We were being hunted and found this church. Ever since we arrived, nothing bad has happened to us."

"Wait," Marcel interrupted, "Nantes is the capital city of Loire. You come from there? How far away is it? Do you know how we can get there?"

"Oh, you don't know? You're in Loire right now. I think the border between the nations is about a day westward. Is that where you came from? Is Ys still standing!? We've been trying to find other people for a long time."

"It seems we've crossed the border without knowing. Yes, it still stands."

"But it's cursed," Dana interjected. "I'm the princess of Ys. My kingdom is cursed and that's why we left. To find help. Tell me, have you ever seen a dragon, or heard of one?"

"A dragon?" Arland thought hard for a moment as he kicked his legs back and forth while sitting on the pew. "I think I remember hearing about that a long time ago, when my parents could speak – back when we still knew other people."

"What else do you know about it?"

"Hmm, nothing really. They said it flew to the south, to the ocean. That's all I remember. I was really young then."

"To the Silver Shore?" Ru asked as he continued to peer at his enemies through the window.

"Yes, sir! I think that's where they said it went."

Marcel asked, "do you happen to know which way that is? South? Can you direct us?"

"Yes, of course. A long time ago, my parents said, the stars and land changed, and evil overcame the world. Everyone had to relearn the world and their place in it." The brown-haired boy stood up and pointed out the window to the stars. "Do you see that group of stars? If you look at it upside down and reverse it, it looks like a saucepan."

"Hm?" Marcel jumped up with eyes of wonder.

"The bright star underneath used to point north, from what I was told, but now it points south."

"Damn!" Marcel erupted with anger. "I thought it was still pointing north."

"And?" Peter asked.

"I've been going in the opposite direction of the star this entire time, but instead of going south we've been going north. That's why it's taken so long for us to cross the border. I should've followed the stupid star the entire time."

The boy laughed and walked over to Dana and sat next to her. "Your friends are funny, Miss Princess. I like them."

"Marcel? My friend?" Dana stopped for a moment and then joined the boy in laughter. "I guess that is kind of funny."

"Hmph." Marcel shrugged. "At least we have an idea as to where to go now." He returned to his seat. "We'll go first thing in the morning when those damn dogs leave."

"Arland," Peter began, "What do you mean when you said, 'when your parents could speak'? What exactly happened to them and Loire? You see, Ys has been cursed for a long time, no one can enter or leave it, with a few exceptions of course. So, we've been a bit out of the loop on these things."

"My parents?" Arland looked over to them. The couple were playing with the flickering flame of the candle, as if amazed by the heat and light. They repeatedly brought their hands close to it, only to get burned and pull it away as if they were entertaining themselves. "Loire was a country that had a religion where there was a God for every single thing. Like one for the Earth and the Sun. But once the evil came, there were no Gods to help us. The evil eventually affected us, too, like it did those animals out there. It changed us into what you see in my mamma and papa."

"Pagans… So, how did you not become like them? You had no one to protect you."

"Well, it didn't happen suddenly, once Nantes was destroyed by the monster and we began to live off the land, that's when the transformations really happened."

"But, why not you, lad?"

"We came across a traveling priest. He baptized me but my parents still had faith in their gods and refused his blessing. He told us of his church where we would be safe and led us here. It took us a long time to arrive, but after I met that priest I never changed. Yet my parents began to change. Slowly they transformed into what they look like now. They became angry and distrustful and they – they…"

"Killed him," Marcel stated abruptly.

Dana could tell that Arland was about to cry and so she held him dearly. "Be kind," she sternly instructed Marcel. "So, little one," she continued as to get the boys mind off his heartache, "what exactly do you do here for fun?"

"Oh, well, I play with my parents a lot during the day. They are not like they used to be. But I spend most of my time looking for food."

"That's very responsible of you! Taking care of your parents like that. You're a good boy."

"Yeah! And at night, I read a lot."

"And what do you read?"

"This!" Arland stood up and rushed to a bookshelf and brought forward a worn-out volume that he presented with a smile.

"What book is this?" Dana held the hardback close to the candle and red aloud the title "'The Book of Enoch'?"

"I think it's a book about religion. I found it here. It talks about weird things like God's Grace, miracles, and angels. I don't understand most of it, but I wish it was true. I could really use a miracle."

"I'm a fantastic reader. Would you like me to read it to you?"

"Yes! Yes!"

"Come here then," Dana beckoned to her lap and the boy laid down and listened intently. She noticed Marcel was eyeing her intently. Perhaps, she figured, he feared what truths the book might hold. She read the words aloud, at least all that was still legible since it was an ancient script. Most of the text was rather cryptic and apocalyptic even, but what really caught her attention was the passage about God's Grace. It read:

"'And when God created man, He instilled in him a part of His own essence. Purity and righteousness, which always connected man to Him. A power to pull from when faced with evil. The will to overcome.'" Dana petered out as she quickly remembered what happened before when facing the Nephilim. In that moment, when she faced the woman, she felt something come from her – and she felt connected to something powerful. *'When that power came from me, was that God's Grace?'*

"More..." Arland demanded.

"'Servants of God, through His eternal Grace are capable of miraculous feats such as receiving visions or altering reality. But most importantly, they can use their abilities to destroy and remove all evil and its effects; whether it be a curse or an evil entity. Those who are close enough to God in this respect are referred to as Saints.'" The text became illegible for a bit, but she read on what was left, "I have been given the duty by God to record the history of my kind and their battles with The Watchers...'" The text came to an end as the rest of the volume was too smeared and faded to read. She looked down at the child to find him sound asleep.

"Some bedtime stories," Marcel sarcastically snickered.

"Whisper." Dana quietly replied.

"I'm going to get some shut-eye, too," Peter said as he stood up and began to walk away.

"As am I," Marcel stated. "What about you, Ru? The young boy seems to have taken your place. But then again, you two don't sleep together much anymore. Why is that?"

Ru left the room, as quiet as he already was. Dana had purposely been avoiding him these last few days ever since the incident. She wasn't sure if their relationship was just or if it was sinful. She also knew that he hadn't been sleeping much ever since. The nightmares kept him awake and the two had been argumentative ever since. Dana responded to Marcel with whatever retort her tired mind could muster, "and you didn't get taken to the nephilim by the vines. Why is *that*?"

Marcel smiled, stood up and said, "from what you tell me of the demon, she'd have nothing to gain from me eating the fruit." And then he left to sleep.

Dana noticed Arland's mother in the corner of her eye, laying next to her sleeping husband, attempting to comb her knotted up, dirty hair. Dana felt sympathy for the woman and called her over. Hesitant at first, the woman saw her son sleeping in Dana's lap and then followed. Dana petted her hair until eventually the mother came to an understanding and Dana began to braid her hair for her.

Dana became lost in thought as she helped the mother with her haggard locks. *'I know I mustn't be cruel to him… I don't want to be. The amount of people I care for is becoming ever so slim. None of this is his fault. But I just can't bring myself to explain it. I'm so weak. So pathetic. I couldn't save Julia and now I'm losing him. If only I was strong enough to keep the people I…'* She stopped from completing the thought – to admit that feeling - that emotion, was not something she was prepared to do. For if she did, she knew she would get lost in it and lose perspective on her mission. She needed to know what the power that came from her before was. Was it God's Grace? Was it truly a miracle? She wasn't sure. She wasn't sure about anything. And focusing on her feelings for Ru was serving to be a distraction. Eventually, after finishing braiding the mother's hair, she fell asleep.

Dana jumped at the sound of Arland's cheering and Peters shouting as she abruptly met the morning. The sun was shining through the windows as everyone, including Arland's mother and father, stood outside and watched Ru as he drew his sword and faced the wolves who did not leave once day broke. Dana joined Peter at the front of the church as he called to her and Marcel.

"C'mon everyone! Let's help him, the fool thinks he can take the giant beasts by himself."

"No, old man," Marcel said. "I'm sure he can handle himself. We'd probably just get in his way."

"Dana?" Peter questioned her but she did not respond.

She watched Ru as he entered the fray with his gleaming, golden sword, gliding through the wolves' offense and slashing them at every chance he got. Not only was he faster but also stronger than the beasts and it was only a matter of time before each and every demonic dog was dead. Ru, who was covered in blood, returned to the church. He did not look at her as he passed by, but instead he approached the boy. But just as it seemed he was to speak, Arland's parents took the boy into their arms and kept him away. Fear was in their eyes once more, fear of Ru. He looked at the blood on his hands and then turned away. He spoke softly, "you can leave now. The wolves won't hunt you anymore."

Arland managed to get some words out from between his cowering parents, "thank you, sir, but it wasn't the wolves that hunted the people of Loire. It was the giant."

"Hm?"

"Yes, he roams this country to kill every human. You should be wary of him."

"We will be," said Marcel as he came forward with their things. "We'll be going now, boy. Are you lot ready? Let's go."

Ru followed swiftly as did Peter, who kept murmuring about Giants as he left. Dana turned around and faced the family and said her final piece, "thank you for letting us stay the night, Arland. I...hope you find your miracle..."

"I already have! Mister Ru left us with a lot of meat to eat!" The boy pointed towards the dead wolves at the front of the church. Some of Ru's blood must've splattered on the animals for they transformed into their normal, edible state. "We've been starving. Please thank him for us!"

Dana smiled and said, "I'll be sure to do that."

CHAPTER NINE

The days of frustration and awkward silence between Ru and Dana continued as Marcel led the party on the corrected path to the Silver Shore. As they crossed wide plains and traversed great valleys, they found themselves in a dried-out gorge just beneath a mountain. They inspected the place for safety and found that it had a split path. The gorge, where the river used to be, eventually ended in a drop where a waterfall must've been. To the left was a path up the mountain and to the right, a small opening into a cavern which, upon further inspection, seemed to continue down into the earth. They decided to return to the center of the gorge and rest for the night.

As the flickering stars illuminated the sky above, the others, except for Marcel, merely had their eyes pinned to the ground and were in no mood for talking or laughter. They sat surrounding a dim, weak fire that offered even less heat than it did light.

Marcel broke the silence, "this is a safe spot. The walls will protect us." There was no response and he continued with a more personal comment, "Dana. The necklace you're wearing, it shimmers from the fire's light. What bird hangs from it?"

"I-I don't know. It was my mother's. I didn't get much of her things when she passed except for this…" She replied.

"It's an Albatross," Ru interjected. "That's the type of bird. I recognize it for whatever reason."

Dana replied with a simple acknowledgment and then looked away.

Ru could overhear Marcel whispering to Peter, "I hate this silence. I know something more happened in that forest than what you've told me. These two were so close before, but now they don't so much as look each other in the eye."

"I thought you'd be happy about it?" Peter replied. "Your side has claimed another. Rather, shouldn't you be focused on something else, like finding us the right path?"

"Hmph, worry not, all." Marcel spoke aloud once more, "we are getting closer. Although this gorge is empty, we must simply follow it down and eventually we'll reach the ocean." He was met with no reply.

Suddenly the earth quaked and shook with several mighty tremors – this had been a common occurrence since they left Arland and the church. Every now and then, in succession, several small but loud tremors would randomly happen. Yet nobody in the party could figure out why, although they had their suspicions. Marcel suggested that it might have been an earthquake, which Peter believed it most likely due to the ever-changing landscape caused by the curse which afflicted the land. The fire nearly collapsed in on itself as the earth quaked and Dana, too, fell over onto the ground after being knocked off balance. Quick to act, Ru leapt to her aid and helped her up. As she looked up at him, rather than thank him, a sadness crept over her face and she shrugged herself away from his grip and returned to her seat, turning away.

Ru had grown upset, frustrated at the situation. He quickly left the fire and found solace in solitude amongst the cool dark forest. *'I guess she hates me now. She won't sleep with me anymore and now the nightmares haunt me every night. Because of what Julia said, she must think getting closer to me is the wrong thing to do. Evil, even. Julia only encouraged her to get closer to me after she ate the fruit. Maybe Dana thinks I'm a devil as well... Maybe I am.'* He sat atop a thick branch and tossed a handful of acorns into the dark. *'None of them can see in this dark as well as I; I can tell that much. When I'm wounded, I scale over like a Wyvern. My blood seems to be of magic, which is evil. My strength and speed are much more than that of anyone else's. And worst of all, I've been of no help to anyone. I thought I could protect them, protect Julia. But I guess I didn't know just how weak I was...just how weak they are. What's the point in this anymore?'*

He stopped throwing the acorns and simply fell asleep on the branch. He didn't care if he fell off.

He awoke to the cries of Dana and the others. As soon as he opened his eyes, through the trees, he could see what appeared to be a giant human moving into the gorge. This must've been the giant Arland warned them about – the one that destroyed Nantes. The shaking of its footsteps knocked Ru off balance causing him to fall onto the ground where he landed on his knees. He quickly acted. He unsheathed his sword and ran towards the giant as it swung its muscular arms into the stone walls and pulled out boulders. As it reeled back to throw them at the three cowering in fear, Ru ran up behind the twenty-foot-tall man and sliced his achilles tendon with a mighty slash. Ru was surprised at just how thick the giant's skin was, it took all his strength to get a clean cut.

The giant fell backwards and onto Ru, causing yet another great quake. It howled in pain as it held its ankle, then stood up and looked down at Ru, who had been crushed into the ground because of the giant's immense weight. There he laid suffering and in a daze; before he could move, the giant yelled out to him, "damn you humans! I will kill you all!" The being then picked Ru up by his foot and slammed his body against the stone wall, cracking his skull open and leaving him for dead. Ru was just barely conscious as he laid on the ground and could only watch as the giant turned towards the three, hobbling, and picked up a boulder and threw it at them. They began to run away, Marcel picked Dana up, in order to move her quickly, and took her inside the cavern. The giant threw yet another boulder after them, which only served to block off its entrance. Peter diverged to the left, up to where the path split and led up the mountain, hoping to lose the giant on its narrow trail.

Ru could feel his scalp scaling over, healing, and his vision returning to him. He found the strength to stand and swiftly he ran towards the giant, jumped up its body with several mighty leaps, and cut off its ear. As he fell from its shoulder, the giant shouted out in pain and smacked Ru in mid-air, sending him half a mile away; all the way up to where Peter hid, breaking several of his bones upon impact. Peter jumped from out of the bushes and came to Ru's aid, pulling him aside.

"Ru! Ru, are you alive?" Peter desperately asked.

Ru looked up at him, shell-shocked and bleeding from his nose. He could barely move. The giant from below shouted, "I see you!" And began to pursue them.

"Come on!" Peter lifted him up, "we got to go!" Ru rested on Peter's shoulders as the two stumbled away, further up the mountain path.

Evening settled and Peter had used all his strength. Ru could walk well enough on his own and sat away from him, looking discontent. After checking the path behind them and in-between catching his shallow breaths, he found the energy to speak to Ru, "are you well? Healed up?"

"Yes," Ru replied, looking away.

"I…think it may be resting, as well. I think the damage you did to its foot is causing it some problems." He paused for a moment to read Ru's reaction, yet it hadn't changed. "I didn't think it would keep following us all the way up. Ah, it's getting cold." Ru continued to look melancholy and Peter couldn't figure out why. "Speak already!"

"Hm?" Ru finally turned to face Peter and spoke softly, "yes, cold."

"Where do you think that thing came from? It must've been following us for days."

"What difference does it make?" Ru replied. "What's the point in any of this suffering? We're running for our lives for what?"

"What do you mean?"

Snowflakes began to fall from the cloudy sky and the temperature drastically dropped. Another effect of the strangeness of the land.

"I can fight for you, I can bleed for you, but ultimately, what for? Eventually, we all end in sin anyways. Maybe the people of Ys deserved what happened to them. Perhaps, they wanted it to happen. I guess that's the nature of man…"

"What the hell is wrong with you, Ru? You've picked a bad time for this." A mighty roar followed Peter's statement and the shaking of the mountain told them that the giant was on the move once more; ever dedicated to their destruction. Peter stood up and began to run off, thinking Ru was following closely behind him. It took him a moment to realize he wasn't. "Come on, lad! What are you doing!? Let's go!"

Ru sighed and sluggishly went along up the frosty mountain.

CHAPTER TEN

Dana kept her distance from Marcel as the two wandered the tight and winding hallways of the muddy cavern. Unfortunately, the darkness forced her to keep somewhat close as she didn't want to be lost and alone, despite how much she distrusted the man in front of her. She'd been at wits end since the giants attack and hadn't rested since. From what she figured, it may have been a day or two since the incident. She couldn't stop thinking about Ru, whether he was alive or not. *'I did it again,'* she thought as her hand passively caressed a jagged wall. *'I ruined things again with another person I care about. Who knows if I'll be able to say I'm sorry and tell him that I-'*

"Ow!" Dana took her palm and saw that her finger was cut by the wall. She put it into her mouth to suck on it, hoping it would seal soon.

"What's wrong?" Marcel turned and looked up at her; the only path in the cavern led downwards.

"Nothing."

"You're tired? You need to rest?"

"Do you?"

He smirked, turned away, and continued. Dana wanted to limit all interaction with him. The last person she wanted to be stuck with was her sister's right-hand man. The two continued for about half an hour more until Marcel spoke again, "here. We're resting here for the night." Marcel led her into a small crevice where a small fragment of light found its way through the earth and dimly lit the room. In the corner was an ample reservoir with hot water that seemed clean enough to drink. Marcel filled some canteens they brought with them and then said, "you can bathe if you wish. This isn't acidic like the other puddles we've come across." Dana looked at him in surprise and disgust. "Don't worry, I won't peek. That puffy hair of yours is off-putting. If the bath will do you good, then do it. I can tell you're exhausted. You need to get rest somehow because you're slowing me down." He sat away from the steaming water, turned in the other direction, and pulled out his sword and began to clean it.

Dana took off her clothes cautiously and entered the hot water. "It's so humid in here – that's why my hair is like that."

"I don't care."

Dana submerged her entire body and found the bath to be quite relaxing. Feeling bored, there was only one thing she could interact with.

"Do you think he's alive?"

Marcel sighed and responded, "of course. I'm sure you know something like him wouldn't be killed by that. It would take much more…"

"Something you've thought long and hard about, I'm sure."

"It wasn't my idea; it was your sister's. But I'm glad we finally get to talk like this, since he isn't here. Being Dahut's servant has its benefits. Unlike you, I do not suffer from the curse of silence and can speak all I wish. When he meets the dragon, I'll help him slay it and then my dream will come true." The wiping of his sword became audible.

"And what dream is that?" Dana asked.

"Your sister will be mine and mine alone."

"You wish to be king? You don't actually think she'll give you any power, do you?"

"King?" Marcel laughed. "I don't want to be king! I want her. All of her. She will be mine. She's spread around and shared. But now she'll be under my thumb. To be crushed or to be spared? But forever my possession."

"Wow, I suppose you two really deserve each other."

"Don't mock me!" Marcel shouted as he turned to face her.

Dana was surprised and quickly dipped her body below to cover up. His face was flustered and frantic. He was in a craze. For the first time ever, she feared him. "I-I wasn't mocking…" He turned away and continued to his blade. A moment of silence passed until she spoke again, "I'll stop him from killing the dragon."

"How can you when you can't even tell him the truth?"

"I'll find a way!"

"And while you do that, I'll be helping him kill it! Afterwards, there will be no curse or conflict. Just bliss. The only reason why I've kept you and the old man alive up to this point is because without you, he has no drive – no purpose. I need him to believe the dragon is evil and to kill it for those he cares for. After that, you lot won't be safe. Don't forget that."

Dana got out of the water and put her clothes back on. She found a decent spot to lay on and attempted to fall asleep; yet she couldn't keep her eyes off of him. She dared not to turn her back on him.

"You needn't worry," Marcel spoke. "As long as I need you, you're sa- did you hear that!?"

"Hear what?" Dana replied.

"Did you hear that voice just now? It's the same from earlier, the one that led me to this room."

"Are you insane? There is no voice."

Marcel looked outside into the dark cavern and returned. "It must be my imagination. I'm going to sleep. Don't think about running away."

Dana fell asleep fearing for her life, alone and wanting. *'Where is Ru?'* She thought to herself.

Marcel hadn't spoken since that night. He simply walked silently at a fervent speed as Dana clamored behind him. She had given up trying to converse with him. He eventually stopped as they came to a sudden drop off. Marcel slowly descended first, and Dana followed as she scraped her gentle skin on the rocks. The air at the bottom was cooler, lighter, even. However, the path forked. Dana felt that the path to the right seemed to have a breeze to it and some light as well, while the left had the exact opposite.

"Let's go this way," Dana suggested.

Marcel ignored her and continued into the pitch black. *'Something is wrong with him... This is my chance to get away!'* The two separated and as she began to flee, she heard Marcel crying out. She hesitated. To run away or to help? Her conscience got the better of her; she turned and ran to his direction.

"Marcel! Marcel! Where are you?" Dana shouted as she fumbled in the dark. She desperately sought his response until, in her periphery, she saw a flicker of light. She followed it and entered a crevice to find a small room. Two torches hung from the wall and on the opposite side, behind what looked like a series of thin stone prison bars, shined a pair of yellow eyes that glowed in absolute darkness. The eyes which were focused singularly on Marcel, now penetrated her very soul. She, too, let out a shriek of terror.

The two men faced a dead-end at the summit of the mountain, and a blinding blizzard with knee-high snow slowed their traversal significantly. Peter was passed out – his old age caught up with him, and the freezing temperature taken its toll. Ru had been carrying him on his back for the past day until he ultimately fell to his knees in exhaustion. A great desperation overcame him after not seeing a path to escape. They were still running from the bloodthirsty giant whose single-minded hatred was Ru's current bane. Yet, he could take no more. As he rested in the snow (and perhaps because of the noise of the blizzard), he didn't hear the giant getting as close to him as it did – and quickly the monster snuck up behind them and smacked the two several yards away.

The pain added on to the struggle of the last several days, and Ru finally met his breaking point. Like a cup that runneth over, he felt overburdened, and the culmination of all the death, pain, loss, and aguish, overcame him. As the giant readied its bawled fists for one final blow, Ru looked up towards it, on his knees, and submitted. He closed his eyes as the fists came to crush him.

A moment passed. And then another. He could feel the heat from his breath warming his face. Ru opened his eyes to see the giant's fists inches before him – stopped in midair. He stumbled backwards and moved about to get a better view of it; he found that the creatures' eyes didn't follow him. He noticed that the giant didn't move at all and it didn't seem to be by choice either, the veins protruding from its mighty arms made it clear that there was still intent within the beast. Upon further discovery, Ru found that within a range of about half a mile, everything stopped - almost as if time itself had frozen in this blizzard of hell. A great warmth filled Ru and his energy returned to him, relaxing his mind, and putting him at ease. A blinding light shined and from nowhere, a person came to be. The ice melted in his presence.

"Do not fear, Ru, for I intend you no harm."

"What are you?" Ru questioned. "What's happened?" Ru raised his sword at the man.

"My name is Enoch. I am of your kind, but not with you." The man wore a simple shroud around his body, and he glowed a golden tint. His hair was wild, but it never seemed to mark his face.

"I've heard that name before… Make sense now or prepare to die." Ru steadied his hand.

"My apologies, I simply forgot that you don't remember me as well as I do you. I am not any enemy of yours. This creature here, the giant, is a male nephilim. He is the brother of the female you met back at the garden. The last of their kind, he bitterly hunts down any human he can and kills them. Out of spite, or revenge, jealousy…perhaps all three. He was the one that destroyed the country of Loire. Yet, I must say again, I intend you no harm. As you can see, I've no weapons."

"I don't think somebody that could stop time would need a weapon such as a sword to kill me…and that if you wanted me dead, you would've just let the giant do so. Yet, it seems you've healed me in some way. Why?" Ru sheathed his blade.

"I was ordered by someone, that if you lost your way, I would help put you back on the correct path."

"Who? The Devil? If so, leave me be and let me die."

Enoch looked perplexed for a moment and then replied, "I see. They have confused even you. How fallible we humans are. No, my friend, I do not know the Devil and neither do you. Marcel has merely been toying with your mind out of sheer hatred and jealousy. I doubt even he knows how much his words have affected you."

"He has? And…you say you're human? Impossible. No man is capable of such power."

"Only through God's Grace can I achieve such feats. Now, you know who I come from. Unfortunately, I was given rather vague instruction, I suppose it is up to me to figure out how to help you. I wonder if that was by design?"

"I'm growing tired of this."

"I shall explain to you what I think I am allowed to and help you restore your faith in humanity, as I think that is what's for the best. I still see hope in our kind, after all."

"Restore my faith? There is none left to restore."

"We will see, but first, let me explain who I am. Look here into this cloud," Enoch removed a sleek, yellow cloud from his sleeve, stretched it out to expand it and turned it to face Ru. It was very similar to a piece of parchment. "In here you will see the past as if it was the present as I narrate."

As Enoch began to speak, several realistic images began to form and move on the cloud, like the things he was saying were actually happening. "Long ago, during my time as an ordinary human, God left several angels in charge of watching over humanity, to guide them and aid them in his stead. There were hundreds, but most notably among them were Azazel and Samyaza. However, these angels, Watchers as they were called, eventually became corrupted by the Devil and sought to overthrow God. In their sin, they mated with humans which bred the nephilim and brought to humans forbidden, evil knowledge thus corrupting mankind even further. Do you understand so far?"

"How did mankind originally become corrupt?"

"They ate the fruit from the tree – the very same one you rejected."

"But not Julia."

"No, like I said, humans are fallible, but we will return to that later. During my time, I was a pious man and chronicled these events dutifully, and as a result, God took me from this world and brought me to live with him, without having to ever face the punishment of death – God's punishment for us having eaten the fruit. My descendants, who were righteous as well, were warned of God's plan to rid the world of the evils of the Watchers and their children and the evil humans that bred with them."

"How did he do that?"

"He advised them to build a giant boat that would carry themselves and all of the animals, because he was to flood the Earth."

"He killed everyone!?"

"Yes, except for these two Nephilim that managed to survive. The Watchers, fallen angels that weren't killed, were imprisoned in Hell for all eternity. The water then receded, and God promised mankind he would never flood them again, and since then, humans have prospered. And that is all I can tell you. I serve God – I enforce His will. He told me before you were even born that if you were to fall from your path, to correct you. I've been watching you since you left Ys. But lately I haven't been agreeing with Him on certain things…"

"And you only now intervene?"

"You were never going to die before, and I knew you wouldn't eat the fruit."

Ru turned away and laughed, "for somebody who's been watching me so closely, it's amazing how little you know." Ru stopped and spoke sternly, "I was going to take the fruit."

Enoch did not reply.

"Ever since then," Ru kicked the snow, "It's all gone to hell! I thought I could save them – help them. But I only led Julia to damnation. If only I could've given her what she needed, but by the time I got her food, it was too late. And the fruit, I was going to eat it, Enoch! I was!" Tears began to form in his eyes. "I would've done anything to save her."

"Dana."

Ru nodded and continued, "But now, because of what Julia said to her, she thinks it… Us, to be evil. I never got the chance to tell her that I never intended to go that far. For sex… I know that outside of union it is wrong. But now she hates me, and I've lost her forever. I have nothing left, Enoch." Ru looked at Peter, who was as still as the giant and presumed dead. "I have no faith. Humans fail so easily, so much so that the Devil can corrupt their entire civilization. And one by one they all fall. The last of the pious ones are dying around me. It must be all my fault – I must be as Marcel said, a demon. It would be better for them if I wasn't around. Why was I even brought into this damned world? Even I can tell, Enoch, that I'm no human. Look." Ru lifted his shirt to reveal the scales growing over his torso.

Enoch held out his hand and rested it on Ru's shoulders. "I truly am sorry that you've been lied to so severely."

"What?"

"You were brought into this world prematurely, so innocent and without sin – you knew nothing of its evils. There was no way to prepare you. I wish I could tell you everything, but it isn't my place. My purpose is only to correct your path by restoring your faith. But what I will tell you is that you are no demon, I can guarantee that."

Ru looked up to Enoch, his sorrow somewhat staved. "How?"

"Now I will restore your faith."

The cloud began to move once more and to Ru's surprise, showed Dana and Marcel in a small underground chamber facing off against something truly sinister.

CHAPTER ELEVEN

Dana was frozen with fear as the yellow eyes fixated on her and Marcel. Whatever creature was in the cavern, behind what looked like a weak and rudimentary cell, emanated a demonic aura. It was a feeling familiar to that of the center of Ys. The being's eyes had no pupils, no iris, just a simple yellow glow that eerily enraptured her. Eventually, whoever was behind the cell, spoke, "ah, the cattle have come out to pasture."

The voice sent shivers down her spine. It was a raspy, high-pitch voice, the kind that would make anyone quiver. She began to feel sick as a thick miasma began to expel from the creature and taint the freezing, crisp air. Her heart felt heavy, like a hand was grasping it, and she began to breathe with great difficulty as sweat fell from her brow. Marcel, from what she could see, was suffering similar effects. The voice continued, "my master told me my salvation was coming. And to think, you would bring me a heifer as well...!" The eyes focused on her when he said this. "Our Lord is quite generous, is He not, Marcel?"

"H-h-how do you know my name?" Marcel spoke, obviously in great fear.

"Our master, Satan, sent me visions that you would be coming. And I have led you to me – it is my voice that you have been hearing since you entered the cavern. You see, I am a servant of His and as a human, that makes you a servant of mine."

"W-who are you!?"

"I am Samyaza – long ago, I, an angel, served the master in rebellion of God. We were defeated and I was sentenced here for all eternity. Yet *He* has sent you to free me. You see, He will rise again soon, and He will need my power to win the upcoming battle. That is, as you know, Dahut's plan and purpose in all this. She will bring Him back upon your mission's completion, and I am to help quell any rebellion from Heaven or from the humans. Do you understand?"

"Yes…but why can't you free yourself? Those bars are fragile and weak. Someone as mighty as you could break them."

"I would have done that long ago if it was so simple, little one. They are blessed by God and upon touch they would destroy me – as would that key over there."

Marcel looked upon the rock next to him and on it laid a simple, small key, that fit the lock to Samyaza's cell door.

"I cannot touch it – but a human can. That is what you are needed for. Do it." Samyaza's eyes flickered blue and Marcel suddenly became quiet and limp. His arm outstretched towards the key and grasped it. He walked towards the cell door. "Good, good. What an obedient dog you are…"

"Marcel! Stop!" Dana broke from her paralysis and shouted out. "Don't do it! He's evil, he won't keep his promise. He'll kill us all! We're nothing but cattle to them. They'll kill you and Dahut once they have no use for you." Marcel did not stop, he slowly approached the door and held out the key to the lock. Samyaza began to chortle a horrifying laugh. "No, stop! Marcel, I won't let you. I won't let any more evil into this world!"

Suddenly, Dana began to shine a pure, white light. She could feel her hair flow wildly in the air and a gentle warmness surrounded. She held out her hand towards the key and as she did, it grew red and Marcel's skin began to sizzle. The knight jerked back, and the key fell to the ground, melted, and dissolved into nothingness.

"No!" Samyaza screamed. "Damn you, wench!" A red, leathery hand, with long black pointed nails, stretched out far in-between the bars and aimed towards her with killing intent. As soon as it came to her, however, the glowing white aura surrounding her repelled it and flung it all the way back into the darkness. Dana couldn't tell what was happening. In this moment, something deep within her, within her heart, was manifesting itself into the world. All that she felt was love. Love for her people, for her friends, and for Ru. And she would use that love to protect them. She felt something similar before, when she faced the nephilim as she was tied to the tree, yet to a lesser extent.

"Aagh!" The fallen angel screamed in pain. "What is this!? I remember it well. The Holy Spirit! She is one with God, I cannot touch her. You!" Samyaza spoke to Marcel, "kill her! She is of no use to us any longer. You will tell Ru it was the dragon that did it and he will believe you and he will seek revenge."

"I-I...but she is Dahut's sister. I was to wait until after –"

"Now!" Samyaza's eye's flickered once more and Marcel became silent.

Dana noticed the demon hand Marcel several small things and heard him whisper something she couldn't make out. Marcel pocketed the items, unsheathed his sword, and charged Dana. She felt no fear in her current state until the blade tagged her arm. She screamed in pain and jumped back. The glow that once surrounded her quickly faded away as she turned and ran out of the room, stumbling about, running towards the way she originally intended – hoping for an exit.

Enoch returned the cloud to his sleeve once the two finished viewing Dana's plight.

"I must save her." Ru was reinvigorated. "I can't believe it; I have become so selfish. I forgot the promise I made to her. To protect her – to help her save Ys. This journey isn't about me at all. Someone as powerful as her, with as much faith and strength she possesses. To resist such evil as she has, I must do what I can, despite how weak I am."

"Indeed," Enoch replied. "The weak need the strong as much as the strong need the weak. And together, you'll find, Ru, that they make each other whole. You must go to her. As fast as possible. She is a saint – one who is so righteous that they have been granted power by God. Only she can lead Ys into a new era of peace and to make it prosper once more."

"Can you take me there?"

"I can. However, I cannot."

"Now is not the time for riddles!"

"Let me show you my back." Enoch removed his shroud and revealed several open and bleeding wounds. "I am as human as you, and performing heavenly feats outside of Heaven costs me a great toll. As you may or may not know, the universe for the undivine is a fickle place. For every action there is a reaction. Every time you give something, something must be taken away. My body can take no more. For me to have enough life left to teleport you to Dana and to heal Peter, you must carry some of my burden. You must take back the wounds I incurred by healing you and stopping time."

"How can I do that?"

"You must return to the spot where I once saved you – the giant's fist. You must take that hit as you once were. I will remove the healing of your wounds."

Ru was afraid and looked at Enoch as if he were crazy. "That will kill me! How can I save her if I'm dead?"

"The toll must be paid. If I return time as it was, and there is no one to take that blow, I will die before I can teleport you. You could, I lament, put your friend Peter there. He is not dead, yet. The cosmic toll would be paid. That would be evil, however. What will you do?"

Ru closed his eyes, and in his heart, knew what the right thing to do was. "Is this some sort of test?"

"Is it that obvious?" Enoch replied with a kind smile. "I must know if you have truly returned to the correct path. If you've truly regained your faith, not only in your friends, but also in yourself, which is most important of all."

Ru turned, walked towards the still giant, and kneeled before the fist. He thought of Dana and her conviction in her faith. He resigned with a smile.

His former wounds returned to him, the snow began to fall, and the fist crippled him. The giant, seemingly unaware of its missed time, roared in celebration. It held its hands up high as it shouted, "I did it, I-" It stopped as it saw something hanging from its fist. Ru dangled from its knuckles and having no time to spare, let go and fell straight into the nephilim's mouth and down into its throat.

Once Ru entered the hot, wet and smelly domain, he couldn't figure out what he was doing. He had been so beaten and battered, all he could do was move his arms about and he did so with conviction. He slashed his sword about recklessly, aiming to do as much damage as possible. He could feel the muscles surrounding him constrict and retract as the blood poured over him, to the point where he began to drown in it. He eventually found a hard spot and stabbed it with great volition and fell out to the frozen arena once again. He wiped his eyes and looked up to find a giant hole in the giants' chest with blood spurting from it like a geyser. The creature fell to the ground, fidgeted about, and died.

Enoch stood with a healed Peter and held out his hand for Ru. Ru's wounds were healed and the three stood, grasping Enoch as ordered, and instantly vanished.

Peter was taken aback. As quickly as the frosty mountain disappeared, a cavalcade of palm trees atop a sandy plain surrounded them. Enoch only briefly explained the situation to him before they left, and so he hadn't fully understood the power of the man, who now spoke with a slur, "this is the other side of the mountain, the Silver Shore. Go… Ru, you must be quick. Save her…"

"Thank you," Ru said as he jumped ahead at inhuman speed, down the path towards the beach.

Enoch fell but Peter caught him and held him, unsure of what was happening. He could feel a warm liquid coming from his back and when he looked at his palms, he saw that the man was bleeding. Enoch's warm golden glow began to fade.

"What's happening?" Peter asked hurriedly.

"I am…dying? I did not think it would hurt so much."

"How can this be? I –"

"Do not worry, Peter, for I am merely going back to where I belong. To give, you must first take away… It is the way of the undivine. It is how we express our love. It is how we perform miracles, how I healed you. But before I go, let me remove the curse of silence upon you as my final act." Enoch brought his fragile hands to Peter's neck and a portion of his glow spread to him and broke the curse.

Peter felt a great burden leave his soul and thanked Enoch, "thank you. Now, I can tell him the truth! So he won't kill-"

"I wonder if this is what He wanted…?"

"What?"

Enoch grew pale and cold. A smile passed across his face. Peter prayed for him, and then quickly ran after Ru, hoping to tell him the truth about the situation before anything happened.

The cavern opened to an ocean and Dana ran across the white beach with great difficulty. Her feet sank slightly in the wet sand, slowing and tiring her. She desperately tried to outrun Marcel, who had gone berserk and seemingly wasn't suffering from the same stamina effects as her. She was exhausted – the tide was crashing against her as she ran parallel to the gloomy beach. The ocean was cold, and a cloudy fog hung over it. She tried to veer left and head into the palm trees where she could hide. She knew that since the white aura had taken over her, the curse of silence was broken. She felt it. All she had to do was find Ru and everything would be okay. That's what she told herself as she desperately ran. She didn't get very far before Marcel tackled her from behind.

The two rolled on the sand until he forced her in place with his muscle and weight, pinning her down. A sick smile came over his face, and instead of grabbing his sword, he wrapped his hands around her neck. Dana tried kicking and punching but her strength was nothing against his sturdy armor. Her neck began to hurt and she couldn't breathe. Her eyes began to bulge, and the cloudy sky began to dim. All hope was lost.

A scream from afar brought her back from the brink.

"Marcel!" Ru shouted as he jolted across the sand at superhuman speed. Marcel only barely unsheathed his sword in time to match Ru's attack. The two blades flickered with an electrifying light as Marcel was pushed back several feet by Ru's incredible strength. Dana could breathe once more, but before she could speak, Ru took command.

"Damn you!" Ru shouted as he charged another ferocious attack. He felt nothing but rage at seeing Dana so hurt and was ready to take revenge tenfold. He slashed Marcel with all his might. While Marcel was the most skilled swordsman in all of Ys, he couldn't quite match his incredible strength and speed beyond deflection. The blades sparked every time they met until Ru finally pushed Marcel to the edge of the shore.

Ru could tell Marcel was growing desperate, but he couldn't predict what he was going to do. He figured he'd try to dodge either left or right, to try and get back on solid land and out of the water. Yet as Ru stepped forward, so did Marcel, doing something unexpected. From below came a glob of wet sand hitting Ru in the face, blinding him momentarily. Marcel dodged to his right and swiped his blade at Ru's fingers, cutting three of them off. Ru instinctively jumped aside, as if trading places with Marcel into the water to try and get some distance. He couldn't see – he knew by the time he removed the sand from his eyes that he would have a sword through him. He had lost.

But that didn't happen. Ru wiped his eyes clean to find Marcel looking up at him in amazement. Marcel seemed so much shorter than him. The knight then looked down at his enemy's feet and Ru followed. Ru couldn't believe it; he was standing on the water! Was this effect part of the curse on the land? Or was it something else? Marcel, however, took advantage of Ru's confusion, dropped his sword, and pulled out two small metal wheels from his pocket and slapped one each atop Ru's hands.

Ru snapped back to the battle, but it was too late. Quickly the wheels grew thin and large, and as they rushed up his arms, they pierced his arms through and through with a thousand-pointed spikes – mangling his arms and making them entirely useless. As the wheels flew off, he screamed in agony and dropped his sword. His feet fell through the water and he came to his knees. Marcel stood over him with another small thing he retrieved from his pocket; a short metal stick.

"I knew you were going to come – my ploy worked! Samyaza told me of the change of plans and gave me the weapons! He knew you were watching! Now that she's a saint, you are no longer needed. Dahut will sacrifice her sister and a saint all in one! Such a sin is enough to bring about the Devil in full strength! Your God does not care! He has abandoned you! Against the Devil and his allies your God will stand no chance." Marcel shook the stick and it extended becoming a mighty spear.

"No!" Dana attempted to interject with her broken voice. Peter, similarly, who had just arrived, shouted down Marcel.

Ru was in shock. He wanted to stand. He wanted to fight. He wanted to respond. But he couldn't. Instead, Marcel plunged the spear deep into Ru's side, mortally wounding him. His blood and guts came pouring out, and he fell forward onto the sand as the water behind him violently crashed against his back.

"I win!" Marcel shouted. "I am the best! I've proved it." Marcel looked about in victory, as if searching for a crowd to cheer him.

Dana passed by him and quickly came to Ru's side. She turned him on his back so the two could see eye to eye. Ru's vision became blurry.

"Ru! Ru! It's me, Dana. Can you see me? Can you hear me?"

"...Yes."

"It's going to be okay. I'm sorry. I Lo-"

Slowly Ru held out his hand to her soft cheek and caressed it. "Is that the rain? Or...are you crying? Don't...cry... Dana..." His hand fell and with it he took ahold of the necklace that hung from her.

Marcel came from behind, pulled Dana away, and chopped off one of Ru's arms. "I'll need this to get through the Dracon Lands. You! Come!" Marcel grabbed Dana by the hair and pulled her along. "We're going back to see your sister! And for me to claim my reward."

"Agh!" Dana shouted, "No! Ru!"

Peter pulled out his sword and attempted to stop Marcel, but he was easily kicked away by the larger, younger man and knocked momentarily unconscious. Marcel and Dana left the beach as Ru, who could barely see, felt something from behind, something from the water, pull him in. The fog that once covered the ocean had taken him over. He knew he was dying. He knew he had failed. Suddenly, he saw nothing but darkness.

CHAPTER TWELVE

Embers of consciousness kindled ever so slightly as he felt the nostalgic memory of being in the egg he was born from once again. He opened his eyes to find himself floating in the deepness of a dark green sea. The light from the surface barely managed to reach him all the way down near the sea floor and he didn't want it to. He felt so comfortable, weightless and numb, he felt completely satiated as he was.

The underwater tide turned turbulent – his body was rocked by the current and tossed from place to place. It was as if he was the water itself – ebbing to and fro, until the water came apart and he fell face-first onto the soft, white sea floor that was now exposed to the daylight.

The pain of gravity bore on him as the water surrounding receded drastically all the way to the horizon until it couldn't be seen. It took Ru a moment to remember who he was and what happened. He looked about himself and found his left arm to be severed, his right hand, while clenched, to be missing three fingers and filled with several holes, and his stomach open and gushing a never-ending pool of blood. *'How am I still alive?'* Ru thought to himself, not believing that even he could survive such wounds. From his fist dangled a necklace, a fine silver chain with a bird, an albatross, hanging from it. He then remembered *her* and quickly his mind began to race. *'Where am I? Is she okay?'* All these questions and more flashed across his mind until ultimately, he came to, *'how can I get to her?'*

Something quickly flew by his head and landed on the sandy ground in front of him. He instantly recognized the bird. It was mostly white but with black wings and blue feet – it waddled around and picked at its wings while clacking its long beak and tweeting its high-pitched chirp. As Ru approached, the bird stopped and looked at him squarely. Their eyes met for quite a bit of time until it spread its wings and flew off in the opposite direction.

Putting on the necklace, he then started to run – he could feel it, he knew the albatross wanted him to follow. He ran across the ocean bed and noticed an instantaneous change in the geography as he was trying to keep up with the bird while it flew high in the sky. Several graves began to decorate the path and they were all marked with a cross. Eventually, the entire landscape was covered with them as he went on. The plane was so flat and the sand and sky the same color, it seemed as if the graves went on for an eternity.

Ru heard a thunderous clash and felt a sudden shake. Looking around he saw that quickly the ocean was returning at a rapid pace. He increased his pace as the tidal waves taunted him from behind. He knew he couldn't fight that force and at the same time he didn't know where the bird was leading him. He saw nothing ahead until, ultimately, the fog cleared, and a giant island materialized. The land was protruding from the ground and built around it were thick walls fortifying it from any weapons or intruders. Behind those walls, further atop, Ru could see several ancient buildings. Most notably he saw what appeared to be a magnificent monastery and church at the very peak of the tall island.

He could feel the water rising, lapping at ankles and he was still at least a mile away from the salvation of the island's dry land. The higher the water became, the more difficult it became to run, as with each strike of the tide it knocked him unbalanced. He didn't think he would make it. The albatross circled the island ahead and chirped out as if cheering him on. It wasn't until the water was up to his chest that the ground beneath him sloped upwards, steepened, and he quickly came to shore at the gate of the island.

The water settled behind him and the bird flew further in behind the walls. Ru was surprised, however, that he felt no exhaustion from the perilous run, and still pondered as to how he felt no pain from the open wound in his stomach, which was still bleeding profusely. The wall in front of him had one small opening, which was sealed by a gate, and above it was a sign that read 'King's Gate.' Ru touched the metal bars and they began to retract on their own into the wall as if somebody on the other side of the wall was pulling the lever. Ru crossed the threshold and found no one there. The lever that controlled the crank had seemingly moved on its own.

Now within the city walls, he walked the only path available to him - a small corridor - and listened to the bird's call until he caught up to it again. It flew above a small open space surrounded by bushes and trees – but in the middle of the area silently stood a marble statue of an idealized man with wings. The albatross swooshed down and landed upon it. Suddenly, all life left the creature and its body fell to the ground, dead.

Ru stepped forward to help the animal but as soon as he did, the statue began to shift and shake – its joints cracking as it slowly moved; coming to life. The angelic statue of a man sluggishly stepped down from its pedestal and looked at Ru with vacant eyes. It moved its hand upwards and pointed towards the top of the island – to the church. The being turned and began to slowly lead Ru throughout the town.

Ru followed, not because he trusted whatever the entity was, but because he had no other choice. This was his only recourse. As the statue of an angel trudged through the cobble stone streets, the ground itself cracked at its immense weight. Ru could've easily outpaced it, but instead he took the time to gaze at the unique environment he was being led through. The streets were desolate, and the stones weathered away, as if years of feet clambering over them had worn them down; forcing them to slope inwards. Ru looked upwards at the houses and saw that they too were in a state of disrepair. Some buildings were half-timbered, made of wood and plaster. Others simply made of stone and topped off with tiled or slate roofs. Ru looked through the windows to see if he could find any residents. What he saw shocked him – a skinless man was kneeling on the floor, praying. Nerve endings and muscles exposed; the person was frantically praying as if trying to end its pain. Ru stepped away from the window and investigated other buildings to find several people in a similar state. Ru retreated to the statue and followed it up the cascading stone steps all the way to the monastery.

The statue of the angel continued with purpose as the two walked under several pointed arches and through an arcade until they entered the monastery. It was adorned with large stained-glass windows depicting a dragon surrounded by angels. Pillars filled the rooms as they passed by and Ru was surprised at how much art filled the great halls and arched ceilings. It didn't make sense to him. If in the residential areas below were the only 'people,' then who managed to build this great structure? Surely, he knew, that a person in that condition was not capable of such a feat. Indeed, to him, nothing made sense.

They traveled further through some halls, passing the green and foggy abbey, up some stairs, until they had finally come to the simple church that stood atop the highest point of the island. The statue stopped just before the church's doors, flexed its muscles and spread its wings. As it did, all the marble on its body crumbled and flew away. What was revealed beneath it was a slick and slender man, completely golden and shining. He and his wings flowed elegantly in motion. The man turned to Ru, bowed, and jumped into the air, flying high all the way to the spire atop the church, where he landed and stood motionless. Ru walked up to the doors and entered the church.

The obsidian dragon sat comfortably on a giant globe surrounded by flickering stars. From above shone the magnificent rays of the sun, and below, where Ru stood on white bricks, a great darkness emanated from the cracks. The dragon, with its four legs, magnificent tail and wings, turned to face Ru and looked down at him with crimson eyes. It sighed, squinted and spoke, "you have finally answered my calls. The visions from your dreams. I suppose you are wondering why you are here. The Silver Shore is the place where this realm and yours were connected when the barriers between them broke down. I sent you those visions to help in your return, so I could set you on your intended path. I knew Enoch could not convince you of everything. I merely instructed him to act as my failsafe in case you failed to return on your own. I never intended to fight you, of course. I was simply going to speak to you at the water's edge." The dragon stopped for a moment. "Oh, look at you, what's wrong? Ah, that's right. You've come to kill me, your own father. That explains the fear."

Ru didn't respond. He was frozen. Something about the creature seemed so familiar to him, yet he knew his whole purpose was to kill it. However, Ru had recently been having doubts. What Marcel said to him, before piercing him with the spear, made him question the reality of the situation.

"I don't know what you are," Ru said. "Where am I? What's happening?"

"You, Ru, as I believed you are called, are dead. You were sent on a fool's errand and were betrayed. Ah, if only you weren't so naïve. Enoch did well enough to get you to the shore, however. At least his sacrifice was not in vain. It was a silly plan of theirs, really, to think I would face you in combat. As if I did not know what outcome that could bring... I suppose I should've known better and did it myself..."

The dragon seemed listless and apathetic. The serpentine tail wafted in the air as the dragon tapped its forefinger against its chin. "Listen!" Ru yelled," are you the Devil or not?"

"Do you see this globe below me? It is Earth, the planet on which you and the other humans reside. You recognize it, no? I created it and all else. Hear me for I shall open your eyes – eyes that have been forced to see a world of lies. I am not the Devil. The man known as Mordred, King of Ys, lied to you on all accounts."

"How so? He seemed like a good, honest man."

"Oh! How the pure are so easily deceived. I shall tell you the truth of the history of Ys."

The dragon quickly flapped its mighty, leathery wings and when the force hit Ru, his consciousness fell away from his body and his mind saw things as God saw them.

"Sometime after I rid the world of the fallen angels and nephilim, I rescinded the waters of the flood and promised mankind I would never again do such a thing… Mankind, all though still sinners, flourished as they attempted to be the best they could be; to be as close to my design as possible. One such man was named Arthur, as you can see, and he became king in a place called Great Britain, which is to the north of Ys, across the sea. He was a righteous man, I favored him, as most kings were cruel and brutal. In him, I saw hope for the species. He was one of faith and for his fairness as a king, I granted him a prosperous lineage. I gifted him three sons, Mordred, Amr, and Llacheu."

"Dana's father? King Arthur was her grandfather?"

"Yes. As the three children became adults and expanded their fathers' domain, I gave them land of their own. For Amr, I calmed a volcano, and, on that land, far to the south, he built a civilization named Sodom. For his brother, Llacheu, I fertilized a desert and he also built a prosperous city named Gomorrah. Mordred did not wish to go as far away and stayed closer to his father – to him I rescinded the sea, and, on that land, he built Ys."

"But Mordred told me that the people of Ys themselves reclaimed it with their own wit, with levies and that Dahut flooded Ys… But that's not what you're showing me…I can see it. I've been lied to."

"Indeed. Eventually, my nemesis Satan, a former angel of mine, corroded the hearts of the people of Sodom and Gomorrah, tempted them and turned them against me. He perverted them and they lost all grace – all sense of divinity I granted the species. In disgust and anger, I destroyed them. I erupted the volcano, burning Sodom to cinder. And Gomorrah, I ripped the earth apart and fell them into it and sealed it afterwards. After hearing of his sons' deaths, Arthur fell ill and died. Soon after, Britain fell to the devil as well and I blew them away with a mighty wind. There was only one civilization left…"

"Ys."

"Mordred had kept his faith regardless and his people were just and righteous, especially his daughter, the one you know as Dana. They were my last sliver of hope for the race…"

"What happened?"

"One day, Mordred's daughter, Dahut, was jealous of her sister's beauty and popularity, she ran away from home and got lost in the woods on the outskirts of the city."

"I see."

"On this night, she was alone and afraid. A handsome man with red hair found her and calmed her. As you may surmise, this man was indeed Satan taking human form. He told her everything she wanted to hear, about how beautiful she was, and she became bewitched by him – in love, even. They spent the night together, and on the next morning he offered her fame and power – all she was without. She wanted him and all that he offered. He told her that she could not have any of it unless he was to manifest into the world permanently, and to do that, she had to make the people of Ys like herself, evil and twisted. The more corrupt the people became, the more power he had to manifest into a permanent corporeal being. He supplied her with the means and knowledge to do so, as well as the knowledge on how to build the tower and its purpose."

"What purpose?"

"The tower was mostly built as an afront to me – Satan wanted to prove that he could lead the humans better than I, and having them build such a mighty tower to Heaven would do so, in his mind. He also intended it to be a link between the two realms, so when he waged yet another war, he could have the humans fight alongside him, the demons, and fallen angels."

"And Dahut succeeded?"

"Dahut became a master of manipulation and magic, which she used to turn most of Ys into degenerates and God-hating people, including her father. She summoned the demonic korrigans to be slaves and help construct the tower of Ys. There were only a few that did not fall prey to her wickedness and desire for power."

"Peter, Dana, and… Julia."

"For a time, yes. She used her magic to silence them. I'm sure you've noticed there have been times where they wished to speak yet could not. Such is why they haven't told you this – they've been cursed. Anyways, as the people of Ys fell further and further from grace, I decided to purge them with the very same water I once rescinded. Satan provided Dahut a premonition of the flood and she led most of the people to the tower to escape. When I appeared before them with mighty waves in tow, many still drowned. I cursed them and they changed into what you know as mermaids – they were to kill all those that ventured from the tower. As you can see, the tower stands above the shoreline – so my flooding of the city did not reach them."

"Why did you do that? You killed so many people!"

"I would have stopped. As Dana and Dahut stood upon the cliff next to the tower, Dana fell to her knees and began to pray, offering her life for the salvation of her people. I saw this and was about to give them another chance, until Dahut fell to her knees as well, and prayed to Satan for the very same. And with that, I washed my hands of them. There was no battle between me and Satan. I simply flew to where I am now and left behind the cursed forest that surrounds the city. Sealing them off from the rest of the world."

Ru returned to his body and fell to his knees with great dizziness. "But those mermaids, they were calling for me. You still haven't explained my role in this. Who am I?"

"You are me, as odd as that sounds. After I left the earthly realm, I sealed Ys off from the world and left one final contingency plan to deal with the humans, in case isolating them did not kill them; as I no longer wished to be bothered."

"What plan?"

"I put part of my soul in a human body, gave birth to you, and hid you in a tree. You were never to be bothered until you hatched on your own – no human was ever meant to find you. That's why I cursed the land surrounding Ys. The wyverns were meant to keep humans away from you."

"No...!"

"And when you were hatched, you would be of one mind – to kill all of those that lived in Ys and then to return to me. I designed you to look like the man that once seduced Dahut so she would welcome you into its walls."

"Liar! I'd never kill them! Not the innocent children of Ys nor those like Dana and Peter!" Ru stood up in denial.

"As you are now, you wouldn't. Now I know that. That's why I sent you those visions after you left Ys without accomplishing your objective. You were born prematurely, and your divine orders were not yet set in your brain. Because of that girl, instead of death, your first thought was her act of mercy, kindness, and love. She transferred all of that to you. And because of that, you have failed in your mission and have ended up here, in Purgatory." Ru was silent. He couldn't believe what he had just been told – or he didn't want to believe it. Was he an instrument of death all along? Meant to kill the people he'd sworn to save? God continued, "the mermaids rang the holy carillon to insure you would go to Ys, so you could find and kill the humans. I instructed them so, it is part of their curse to answer to me. Only you of divine descent could hear those bells while they were underwater. The humans could not, but if they could…"

"If they could what?"

"If one was to rescind the water and the bells were to be rung by a saintly person, then the magic that curses the citizens of Ys would be vanquished and they would be freed. Their memories of righteousness would return."

"So that's why Peter wanted to relearn how to make the bells! Why couldn't he remember?"

"I tested Peter. Before Ys fell, I sent him visions on how to create the carillon so he could save his people. But when the time came for him to play the instrument he fled."

"That's not like him. He's a brave and wise man. Why would he run? Why would he need to?"

"To turn the tide, he was to play the bells and face death. A sacrifice must be made to save his people's souls. I believe Enoch told you something of this. Instead of facing death and playing the carillon, he ran to the safety of the tower. I took the knowledge of how to build and play the carillon from him. Humanity does not deserve to be freed from the curse, for it would make no difference. The magic Dahut used on them was only a hex or a suggestion – it did not force the humans to turn to evil. In the end, the species is simply fallen. A mistake I will soon rectify."

CHAPTER THIRTEEN

The midnight sparkle of the stars served only as a reminder to Peter of just how tired he was. As he stood before the lush and stormy forest of the Dracon Lands, he fought his body's urge to rest. On this journey, he found that his age had finally caught up with him and made it extremely difficult to follow Marcel and Dana's tracks as they traveled all the way back to Ys. Although they took an alternate and easier path, Peter was never able to catch up.

He pulled two of Ru's fingers out of his pocket and remembered the sadness he felt when he awoke on the beach and could not find Ru's corpse, but only his fingers and his sword. He figured the tide took his body, and after mourning his friend, moved on to fulfill his final wishes. Peter knew what Ru wanted: he wanted to save Ys; but above all else, he wanted to save Dana. Peter took that responsibility onto his shoulders, as well as Ru's sword, and traveled all the way back to where his journey began. If he couldn't save Ys like he wanted, he would at least save Dana.

Peter held a finger in each hand and took his first steps into the stormy forest. The wisps that haunted the woods quickly sprung from their hiding places and flew towards him to take his body for their own. He held out his hand and closed his eyes, hoping his plan would work. As soon as the spirits came into proximity, they were instantly repelled by Ru's fingers. Not only that, but the intrepid storm was not affecting him in the slightest. The rain fell around him and the winds parted as they nearly struck him. He was nervous as he walked slowly throughout the woods but was happy the plan he stole from Marcel worked, for him at least. In some way, Peter thought, it felt like Ru was helping him from beyond the grave.

As he cautiously walked through the muddy forest and throughout the lonesome journey back, he couldn't help but count his regrets. '*If only we found a way to tell him the truth it wouldn't have come to this. Maybe, if I had taken the fruit, they would've been better off. I would've been damned, but I could've at least told them how to make the carillon. For the loss of my life, I could've saved all of theirs. All of Ys. If he only knew just how important the bells are...*' Peter slipped a bit in the rushing mud and fell on his side, dropping the fingers. A wisp jumped at the opportunity and forced itself into him. "Aughh!" Peter cried out in pain as more began to fly towards him. He grabbed the fallen fingers just in time and the onslaught of souls were repelled. He stood up and continued on his way, lost in thought. *'The carillon had had holy powers to ward off evil. All it needed was a person just as blessed. That's why it was the first thing the king sealed off when he became controlled by Dahut. Her plan, her magic, would've never worked if those bells rang! Yet I was too scared. If only I had another chance, even if it meant my death, I would ring those bells if God would forgive me and gave me that chance. But it's too late for that now!'*

Peter finally exited the Dracon Lands and found himself in front of the bronze gate of Ys and its tall, thick walls. The giant tower in front of him pierced the morning sky. He threw down the fingers and pulled out his sword, leaving Ru's at his waist, and ran towards the gate. He expected to be confronted by soldiers but rather found the gate to be abandoned and even slightly ajar. He couldn't figure out why until he heard the sounds of celebration coming from within the city. The faint beating of drums and cheering echoed out all the way from inside Ys' dense walls. He ventured further in.

The first thing Peter noticed was his home at the base of the tower. His fields of crops were blazing aflame, his animals slaughtered, and house in shambles. There it was; his entire life post-flood had been destroyed. Everything he had built with his own two hands, without the help from the evil korrigans, was gone. He hadn't the time to mourn. He continued up the road to the tower and found the outer walls to be vacant, except for the sounds of cheering and screaming coming from further within. Peter ran through the maze of hallways, running past many korrigans, until he got to the core of Ys. There he saw the entire civilization standing in reckless abandon, on the sidelines, rooting for what was to come. They played music, drank, and fornicated while celebrating the occasion. Atop the stairs was Marcel pulling a chained Dana up the steps while Dahut stood by, laughing next to her frail father. They were headed for the giant door where the citizens sacrificed their children.

Peter acted instantaneously. He brandished his sword and shouted louder than everyone else in the city. "Marcel!" He screamed with intensity. The music stopped and they all stood and stared at him, even Dana, who looked back at him in tears.

"Peter!?" She shouted. "Run! Hurry!"

"Shut up!" Marcel jerked her chains harshly, causing her to fall to the ground.

Dahut commanded Marcel, "how did he get here? Get rid of that pest!"

"Yes," Marcel continued, "you soldiers! Kill that man!" Marcel and the others continued towards the giant door that was creaking open.

The soldiers quickly took to arms and rushed around Peter. He was out matched – they were ten fully armored, young men who were far more capable than him in battle. How was he to get passed them to save her? He could see her far away, being led into the darkness of the sacrificial chambers. Was all hope lost?

Suddenly his eyes began to burn and within his mind he saw several visions of the past, present, and future. Swiftly he pulled out Ru's golden sword, and with all his might, he threw it into the air, as high as it would go.

Ru looked grievously up at his father, the dragon, "rectify? What do you mean?"

"Look here," the dragon drew forth a cloud, much like how Enoch did before, and showed Ru the status of Ys.

"No! Dana!" Ru saw her, chained and tied, being led up the stairs into the inner-most room of the tower, where he'd once ventured. Marcel dragged her along as Dahut and King Mordred walked alongside him, while the citizens of Ys cheered. At the very bottom of the steps he saw his friend Peter holding his weapon, and carrying Ru's as well, facing the entirety of Ys alone.

"Dahut is going to sacrifice her sister Dana. And when she does, I will do what I should've done years ago, and finally rid the world of these ants."

"How is she going to do that?"

"At Ys' core is where he resides. When you entered the tower, and looked down into its depths; you were looking at the Devil himself, and he was looking at you. He simply was not yet ready to emerge; he was not strong enough. His presence in this realm is what has altered the entirety of the planet and has broken down the barriers between Heaven, Earth, and Hell. I only cursed the immediate areas near Ys, not the rest of it. The warped earth you've come to know was due only to his presence. Once she has been sacrificed and he's manifested, he will kill all those who oppose him and rage war upon me again. I will flood Ys once more, this time, I will be sure to kill all of its inhabitants with one final tidal wave."

"What changed about Dana that sacrificing her now is enough to bring him forth? I remember what Marcel and Enoch said. She became a Saint. And only one person, one entity, one God, can grant that."

The dragon did not respond.

"If you've truly lost all faith in humans," Ru continued, "then why bother saving her, not only once, but twice! When she faced the Nephilim, I could see it then, I remember. That flashing light. It was the same light Dana shone when she faced Samyaza, just not as strong. Why do that, Father, if you've stopped caring? Why!?"

"I..."

"And you, their Father – their creator, is it not incumbent on you to stand by them, love them, and hold faith in them despite their faults? They are only as perfect as they can be – they are meek and small, beautifully fallen. It is your place – our place, to protect them. But you didn't. At every step, once they failed to meet your expectations, you rid the world of them. It's not that they had no faith in you, it's you who had no faith in them. I won't make that same mistake." Ru turned abruptly for the door.

"Where are you going?" The dragon spoke hastily. It extended its head out curiously as if taken by Ru's words.

"I'm going to save her. I'm going to save all of them. No matter what."

"But you're dead."

"Then give me life."

The dragon became silent for several moments, as if thinking, until it finally spoke, "I suppose you have a point. For you, who is of me, I will give them one last chance. If you can save her and keep the humans from falling even further into evil, I will remove the curse on the land and spare them. But if you fail -"

"I won't. And if you try to destroy them again, then it's me you'll answer to."

The dragon snickered, uncoiled, and stretched its arm out pointing one of its fingers at Ru. He was scared, although he'd spoken bravely, he had no real plan…no solution. God then pierced his nail through Ru's chest and into his heart. Suddenly, Ru began to shine brightly, and a white light overcame him. As the light faded, Ru felt a sudden surge of power flow through him and he felt alive once more. He also felt stronger and taller. He looked down and began to panic.

"Don't fear." God spoke, "look at yourself in this mirror."

The dragon brought forth a reflective cloud and Ru saw that his body had been remade – remade in his creators' image. Everything about his body was strong, thick, and scaled over. His red hair flowed elegantly, and he was muscle bound from his neck to the tip of his tail. His arms had been healed and now his hands had become giant, scaled claws. His feet were long, arched, with three pointed toes. The only thing that hadn't changed was his face, and even then, his pupils had become vertical like those of a cat, and his teeth were slightly sharper than before. From his back shone giant wings of crimson flame.

The dragon continued, "If you had been born at the right time, then once you entered Ys, your body would've made this transformation on its own. Rather, your body has been doing it very slowly and was only forced to do so once you'd been injured. This is your true divine form with all of its miraculous powers included. This is who you really are, your true strength, my son. Now go! Fly to them, save them! In your divine state you can easily cross the barrier between realms. Godspeed, my boy!"

Ru turned fast and with one giant leap broke through the doors of the church and off the cliff of the island into the sky. He had no fear of falling. With a single flap of his flaming wings he burst with a booming sound and the world fell before him. Time and space melted.

He knew his purpose.

CHAPTER FOURTEEN

Ru appeared in front of the tower and his immense speed propelled him to burst through the walls of Ys as he caught his sword thrown upwards by Peter. His new form granted him the ability to send visions and he had sent one to Peter telling him of his arrival. All of Ys staggered below him as they were enraptured at the sight of Ru as he floated above Peter. Yet he had no time to stop – he flew with all his power straight towards the closing door into the sacrificial chamber. He had to save Dana before Dahut sacrificed her! Destroying the wooden door, he illuminated the dark core of Ys with his flaming wings and looked about for the blue-haired maiden. All that he saw was Dahut standing at the edge, laughing, and Marcel looking up at him in amazement. Ru was too late.

He flew down the hole with miraculous speed and saw her in the distance. He could hear her screaming as she fell, which only made him fly harder and faster. With all his might, he strained his wings to surpass her and he caught at the last second, before what would've been a fatal landing. Dana looked up at him.

"Ru…? Is that you? I thought-"

"Don't worry, Dana, everything is all right. I'm here." He let her down and freed her from her shackles. She looked up at him with wide eyes. He removed her necklace from his person and gently placed it around her neck.

"Your body is hard. You're like a -"

"Dragon? I know."

"Ru, did I die? Is that why I'm seeing you? I'm so sorry! There was so much I wanted to tell you." Dana began to cry into his chest.

"No, Dana, you didn't die. I'm here. Alive. And I know everything. God told me, my Father did. But I must apologize to you…"

"Why?"

"Because I didn't stop her in time. Look."

Ru pointed forwards and what he saw disgusted him. Thousands of small arms and legs, swarmed about the bottom of the pit, morphing together into one giant, fleshy ball. It began to float in the air, shaking violently until it took form. Suddenly, giant, muscular arms and legs jolted from the blob, as did a head and tail. Expansive wings grew from the flesh, and eventually the creature finished off its form with black fur growing all over. Ru recognized this creature well. He'd seen it in Mordred's book. The head and hoofs of a goat, arms and chest of a gorilla, serpent-headed tail and wings of a bat. The sacrifice had been a success. The Devil was summoned.

"But it didn't work!" Dana shouted. "I'm alive, you saved me."

Dahut, who was looking down from above shouted back, "it doesn't matter if you actually die! It's the thought – the act itself that counts! I pushed you off with the full intention of killing you, little sister! Now die for real!"

The beast shook and flexed its muscles and looked at Ru squarely.

"Move!" Ru pushed Dana away. The Devil spread its wings and tackled Ru just as fast, if not faster, then Ru himself could move. Satan knocked him straight through the wooden door that led to the long pier at the back of the tower, facing the ocean which sunk Ys a decade ago. Ru skidded along the pavement with the wind knocked out of him, until he used his strong claws to hold him in place. He was amazed at Satan's power and felt incredibly small as the beast shook the ground while approaching him. The Devil opened his mouth and spoke in a deathly voice, "Son of God, I will have you melting in a vault of excrement for all eternity!"

Once again, he jumped for him, but this time Ru was prepared. Ru unsheathed his golden sword and parried the beast's mighty punch, getting behind him to strike his back. Yet little did he know that the Devil's tail had a mind of its own, and as soon as Ru was about to attack, the serpent struck Ru, biting into his neck, and flung him into the wall of the tower, above the doorway he had just been knocked out of.

"Ru! Are you okay?" Dana asked him as she came out from the room.

Ru fell down to her side. "Stay back! I can't fight him if you're around! You're my only weakness. If he gets you, I don't know what I'll do." From the path leading to the front of Ys came the entirety of its civilization, running and clamoring to see the fight. Dahut and Marcel led the pack, with King Mordred standing behind them. Peter ran through the crowd to get to his friends' side. "Peter! Dana! Protect them all while I fight."

"Yes!" Dana agreed, but as she ran towards Peter, the Devil jumped for her.

Ru flew between the two, absorbing the blow with his sword, stopping the beast's wicked attack. "I've had enough!" Ru shouted and he smacked the Devil straight into the ground with a punch to his jaw. "I'm ending this now!" Ru flew downwards with his blade pointed straight towards Satan's gut and pierced him, wounding him greatly. The Devil howled, grabbed Ru's sword, pulled it from his stomach, and flung him several yards away.

Dana came to Peter's side who responded, "how did that not kill it!? He just picked Ru up like he was nothing!"

Suddenly, from the shadows the small and frail korrigans began to swarm out and surround Ru from all sides. "Look out!" Dana shouted.

Satan howled once more and the korrigans began to change, morphing into large, strong, abominations and jumped onto Ru, knocking him off balance. Hundreds of them came from the dark corners of Ys and began to beat him with all their might until eventually, he fell to the ground. The Devil started to laugh, as did the people of Ys.

"No!" Ru could hear Dana say in-between the barrage of fists pillaging his face. He could not allow himself to lose. And then he remembered where he was. Ru's hand started to shine, he held it out towards the ocean and within moments, the once still water rippled with ferocity as hundreds of mermaids jumped out from the depths of the old Ys below and came to his aid. The vicious ocean creatures, with their tridents and harpoons, attacked the Korrigans with a vengeance. As the two species battled, Ru found his way out of the scrimmage and faced Satan once more.

Dahut came to the forefront of her people and commanded of them, "people of Ys! Aid your savior and strike down the mermaids to secure your existence under his reign! Attack! Now!" And by her order, the men and women of Ys picked up whatever they could use as a weapon and charged at the mermaids to kill them. All except for King Mordred, however, who in his fragility and cowardice kept to the shadows observing the fight.

"Stop!" Dana shouted. "Don't you know they are our brothers and sisters? They are simply cursed!" The people did not listen, and they continued their assault on the finned creatures, until eventually, all of Ys was at war.

Ru knew that his battle with the Devil would only get more people killed, so he rushed the Devil, slashing him a few times, and flew up to the top of the tower to be out of the way. Satan fell for the bait, spread out his hairy, bat-like wings and followed.

Peter tried his very best to fight the korrigans, yet every time he did, one of the citizens of Ys would simply get in his way and counter him. He could not bring himself to kill one of his own, no matter how misguided they were. Eventually, he fell back and simply watched as the battle resumed. He saw that Dana was quite capable of defending herself. She glowed with an immense, white aura and was able to destroy several korrigans on her own with the pure light illuminating her. And when any human tried to stop her, she simply used her powers to put them to sleep.

As Peter continued to look about, he saw Marcel defending Dahut from two mermaids. Although he managed to kill both, he had been wounded in the process. Marcel nervously looked at the battle, turned, and took Dahut into a grassy, secluded area behind the cliffs of Ys; in-between them and the walls that were built around the city. Peter deftly followed the two, being sure not to lose them in the chaos. He came to find them alone and in argument. He stood in a bush and quietly watched.

"Why have you taken me out here?" Dahut asked. "I should be out there leading them."

"As you can see, my princess, I've been wounded. But worry not, it isn't fatal," Marcel replied.

"What of it?"

Marcel pushed her towards the wall and forced himself on her. "I don't like my odds at surviving this and so I'm taking my winnings early. I hope you don't mind." He began to tug and rip her clothing.

Peter was stunned at the sight of what was happening before him. On one hand, he wanted to stop Marcel, on the other, he knew Dahut deserved worse. He chose not to act, however, as he saw how calm and cold Dahut's face was. She wrapped her arms around Marcel as he began to kiss her neck and a small snicker blossomed on her face. Black electricity expelled from her fingertips and shocked Marcel with a deadly pulse. She was unaffected, but he was left fried and stunned. She effortlessly pushed him onto the ground.

"I knew of your obsession since I was a child. I've used that to have you do my bidding for years. What a pathetic little man you are, truly the greatest fool I've ever known. I hope you enjoy Hell, filth." She spat on him and walked away, returning to the battle.

Once she passed by, Peter walked up to Marcel, who had begun to moan shortly thereafter. He stood over him, checking his status.

Marcel looked up and spoke, "y-you. Ha! You're stronger than I thought o-old man…" He grunted as the pain from Dahut's attack ran through him again. "I must say, I didn't expect to see you again after I left you on the beach."

"Why'd you do it?"

"Hm?"

"You could've easily just run and hid. Why risk taking her here and doing that? Surely, you knew she had powers."

"I guess you don't get it… There is no hiding for me. I chose the wrong side. I realized that when I saw Ru flying over me, in all his glory. I knew then…too late…that he was King. The Devil…has no chance… There is no redemption for me. Not for the things I've done. I figured I'd just have my last bit of fun before Ru tracks me down."

"You don't have to worry about that."

"I… I don't?"

Peter shoved his sword through Marcel's heart. The black-haired knight struggled for a moment until he breathed his last.

Peter returned to the fight more determined than ever to save Ys.

Dana could feel the power of God coursing through her. She had faith in Him and He in her. She was at peace in her heart with that fact, for if God had abandoned her, she would never have been able to use this magnificent ability. She knew the war between good and evil still waged. Her blue hair flowed wildly as she pointed her glowing hands at the korrigans attacking the mermaids and destroyed them upon contact. She could even do it with thought, much like how she did in the cavern when facing Samyaza. The mermaids seemed to recognize that she was their ally, and only seemed to attack the humans when provoked. Something about them had changed, she thought, whereas before they were volatile towards all humans. She understood that it must be because they were answering to Ru's command and they were doing so because he's...*special.* Something she always knew but hadn't truly grasped. She was far too caught up with saving Ys and her feelings towards him to think logically about his origin. Now that she thought about it - finding him in an egg in the Dracon Lands, and how his eyes looked when she first saw him, and all the other miraculous feats he'd accomplished. It only made sense that he was related to God.

A person jumped towards her, she deflected him with a barrier, and put him to sleep. She continued in deep thought, trying to disassociate from the unpleasantness of the fight. All she wanted, after all, was for God to forgive them and revert things back to the way they were. She was willing to give up her life, once they had arrived at the dragon, to do so; if it came to that. As long as it meant the people of Ys were to be taken back from evil. But along the way, she had come to realize her feelings for the man she'd saved that day and was glad that she hadn't died. She was very happy that she found him not to be dead either; she had something to fight for. She realized Ru was an answer to her prayers in more ways than one.

"Ah!" Dana screamed as a bolt of black lightning struck her from behind. She fell to the ground face-first. She turned around and looked up to find her sister, glowing with a black aura. Dana stood and faced her evil sister. "Dahut!"

Dahut spoke, "he'll kill you next after he's done with your boyfriend. But I'd rather do it myself, once and for all!"

Dahut summoned her magic into her fingertips and shot a blinding flash of lightning. Dana focused all her power into a forcefield, and as the lightning struck, it simply bounced off the round barrier and reflected backwards onto Dahut herself. She screamed a gargling mess of sounds as she was lifted off the ground and vaulted all the way onto a nearby mermaid's spear. The creature threw her down and continued its fight elsewhere. Dana walked over to her dying sister, who was fried and skewered, and said her final piece. "Your pride, jealousy, and ambition were your own undoing. We could have been a happy family, Dahut."

"… And be second to you? Never…"

"How sad…" Dana turned, leaving her sister, and rejoined the fight.

With that, some of the denizens of Ys began to falter, and their faith in the Devil began to waiver. Some were filled with fear and questioned if the Devil could truly win and those who had lived in the outer sections of the city, who were less influenced, began to run away. A few who stayed began to see Dana as something more than a mere princess. They began to see her as a Queen and joined her in the fray.

The two celestial beings floated upon the pinnacles of the unfinished tower staring each other down. Ru flew forwards and swung his blade with a giant arc, but the Devil was faster and punched him in the gut knocking him back. It then took initiative, grabbed one of the spires and began to smack Ru with it several times, until the stone broke across his head. Ru grabbed the Devils arm, maneuvered him, and kicked him into the tower. He flew in after and fought Satan in the kings throne room, slashing at the creature's tendons as he swiftly dodged its giant fists. The snake tried once more to counter Ru's tactic, yet Ru instinctively opened his mouth and exhaled a burning fire that burnt the thing to a crisp. The Devil yelled out in pain and grabbed Ru with both of his hands and began to twist him until his ribs and chest began to crack. Ru used his own tail to smack the beast in the face and then kicked its snout with his mighty, dragon-like feet. Feeling the grip loosen, Ru broke free of his enemies' clutches and fell onto the ground breathing heavily.

Satan had become visibly annoyed and the pain from the wounds of Ru's sword was telling in how much of his black blood gushed out. He lifted his hand and suddenly a giant ball of dark energy manifested from his palm. As it grew larger, so did its gravitational pull. Ru found himself being sucked in, closer and closer, as with all the furniture and light in the room, until he was knocked off balance. Quickly, the demon acted and jumped forward, punching Ru with the giant ball, knocking him through the tower, sending him all the way down to the bottom of the ocean with the sphere of dark energy.

Satan flew out, floating above the water, waiting to be sure if Ru had died or not. Ru could barely see to the top of the water as he was pushed even farther into the depths of the ocean by the black ball. He pushed back as best he could, but eventually his back was against the vacant streets of the ruined Ys of yore. He began to weaken, and his sword cracked, but then he remembered who he was fighting for. Dana, Peter, the innocent, *the world*. His muscles doubled in size and with all his might he repelled the ball and flung it back up to the sky. But it was not without cost; his blade was destroyed in the process – only the hilt remained. He kicked off the ground and flew up, immediately trading blows with the Devil. One punch after another, they fought while flying back to the top of the tower where their battle had begun. They returned to the pinnacles where their bout started; both equally damaged and exhausted.

The Devil began to chortle as he opened his mouth wide. A dark miasma permeated as he stuck his hand into his goat-like maw and all the way down his throat, until he violently pulled out a long, jagged sword. He flaunted it as if mocking Ru's lack of a weapon. Ru was unimpressed. He noticed the sun shining above, pointed the hilt of his broken sword towards it, and willed forth the celestial power. A blade of golden flame emerged, and he brandished it towards the demon, whose smile had faded.

"Let's end this," Ru stated.

The two steadied their blades and once more stared each other down. The still air flickered with a sudden gust of wind and the two jumped. With a single strike they passed each other, each with a deadly wound. They fell down, hitting the towers walls on the way, and landed straight in the middle of the war waging beneath.

CHAPTER FIFTEEN

Ru opened his eyes and saw Dana staring back at him. "What happened?" he asked, as tired as he was. He found that she was looking down at him as he lay in her lap.

"You did it, Ru, you stopped him. Are you alright?" Dana put her hands out to Ru's side which was bleeding terribly.

"Don't look at me like that," Ru said with a smile. "The last time you did, it didn't end well for me. I think I'll be okay; he missed my vitals. This new body of mine is durable." Ru sat up with Dana's help and together they looked at the Devil's corpse, as it lay with a flaming sword through its heart. "The people of Ys have stopped fighting."

"So have the mermaids. And look! The korrigans have run off. Finally! We're free! The evil that curses this place is gone."

The crowd gasped and suddenly Ru's attention was brought back toward Satan. It was not him that was moving, but Dahut who was still barely alive. Quickly, she sped with the rest of her might to the corpse.

Dana cried, "Dahut!? Stop!"

Ru began to stand up, trying his hardest to reach her in time; but his body betrayed him. And before he met his feet, Dahut had already cupped the Devil's black blood within her hands and swiftly swallowed it.

The sky became littered with red clouds and the earth shook terribly. The people of Ys began to scream and run aimlessly. The tower of Ys cracked and started to fall apart – pieces above falling and killing many.

"What's happening?" Peter shouted as he walked up to Ru.

"I failed!" Ru answered, "my father said I had to save humanity from falling even further into evil. But look at her – I didn't save her! I didn't save anyone."

Dahut's skin turned black and her eyes red. Her smile even more wicked, and an evil laughter bellowed from her thin frame. Lightning surrounded her and she began to float above the ground.

"No, Ru," Dana said, "this is my fault. I should've made sure she was dead."

"Some people just can't be saved," Peter interjected. "But what was that shaking just now? What exactly is going on, Ru?"

Ru looked towards the ocean and replied, "it's an earthquake beneath the sea. God said if I couldn't stop this, he would destroy Ys once and for all – by flooding it. Look!"

And just as Ru said, a titanic tidal wave came rushing towards Ys off its shore. Violent and treacherous, eighty-feet high (taller than the tower itself), it came rushing towards them with an undeniable force.

"No!" Peter shouted.

"Ru," Dana said, "what do we do? Has God forsaken us!?"

"No! I won't let this happen – I won't let my people die. I can't!" Ru shouted and his body began to shine brightly. He could feel his body change. The scales that covered his body spread to his face and suddenly his human-like profile became elongated, bones growing and cartilage snapping. In just a short time his body grew just as tall as the wave. His wings, no longer of flame, but of skin and scales. He had taken a form like his fathers; a dragon. Ru flew out to sea and spread his giant wings, cupping the entire ocean, as the tidal wave smacked him harshly. He was pushed back a little, but he steadied his form and tried his very best to repel the wave.

"Amazing!" Dana exclaimed. "He's doing it! He's saving us!" Ru could just barely hear her, even with his improved hearing that his new form granted.

Dahut quickly shot a blast a lightning at Ru's back, causing him to stumble – the water began to weaken him, and he could no longer keep his head above it. Every couple of seconds the salt water would slip through his sharp, dragon teeth and he would breathe it in. From the corner of his eyes he looked towards his friends for help. He couldn't do this alone.

Dana pleaded to her sister, "If he fails, you'll also drown!"

Dahut snickered and replied, "Unlikely! I am now blessed with the gift of flight. If I wish, I can just fly away. But I will have you all perish before I do!"

As Dahut charged another blast, Dana began to glow a deep blue and her beautiful face became filled with sheer determination that Ru believed to be driven by justness and love. She held out her hand and sent a beam of power at Dahut, too, making the two clash in a spark of blue and black.

"How are you doing that!?" Peter asked. "Hasn't God abandoned us? Whose power are you using?"

"It's my own! My grace, for my people and my love!" And her power doubled as she evenly matched Dahut's.

The human onlookers, the ones who hadn't run away, were mixed in who they were cheering for, while the mermaids seemed to encourage Dana.

Peter looked at Ru, as if examining his circumstance and loudly shouted to him, "Ru! Hold the water there for as long as you can! I've got a plan!"

Ru roared in confirmation as Peter ran down the cliffs to the Ys of yore, which had been freed from its watery captors. Containing his

Fathers rage was the hardest thing Ru had ever done and it exasperated him immensely. But he would do it for as long as he could.

Halfway down, Peter slipped off one of the wet rocks and fell several feet onto his back. He ached so fully that for several moments he thought he was dying. But Ru's cries in the distance drove his old and weary body forwards. He continued down the weathered path to the base of the mountain that Ys' tower resided on; and into the original city of Ys. A city once known for its ingenuity, architecture, and art, was now (after many years underwater) rusted and weathered. Peter was dismayed at the sight, yet he continued to his destination.

He ran into the dilapidated cathedral, running past the barnacles and dying fish flopping around. He knew Ru couldn't hold out for long. With all the strength his old body could muster he ran past the pews, up the stairs in the back, and into the upper levels of the building where he found what he was looking for. The room was wide and tall, enough so to fit the twenty-seven cast-iron bells in the ceiling which were attached all the way down to the keyboard below where Peter rushed. He sat down, tried to play, and found that his mind went completely blank. Not only had he lost the knowledge of how to make the instrument, but also how to play it. The carillon was no simple bell that one could ring. It was a complex instrument that took training and talent to learn. He looked at the long set of stick like keys, meant for both the hands and feet and quickly began to panic. How was he to save the people from evils influence if he couldn't remember? He had come all this way hoping that once he sat in front of the bells he would somehow recall how to play; a last-ditch effort.

From the window he saw a flash of lightning and saw that Ru had been struck once more by Dahut. Although he repelled much of the water, what was left overtook him, and quickly he was taken by it, submerged, as it continued its trajectory towards the tower and Peter.

Peter felt remorse for the loss of his friend and his people. He knew he couldn't avoid the oncoming tidal wave. Tears leaked from his closed eyes. He stretched out his hands and feet towards the keys, and in memoriam, struck them with the last of his will, a requiem for the innocent of Ys and all of humanity.

The bells rang in discord, but he didn't notice, he kept striking the keys as his emotions rang through him. All his life and all of his faith rippled through as he moved along, dancing up and down the bench hitting the keys. He was so lost in the moment that he didn't notice the beautiful sound that began to come from the bells above. Eventually he heard the water come in and he opened his eyes: just before the water hit him. He saw that he also glowed with a blue radiance. But before he could make any sense of it, a golden brightness overcame him from a glowing hand, and it swept him away.

The white space was ephemeral and calming. He felt weightless as the man with wings took him to his destination. The man turned his head and faced Peter, revealing his identity. He spoke, "remember, to give you must take away. Remember…"

The next thing Peter noticed was landing on the dock behind the tower of Ys and seeing a shocking sight.

Peter had just descended the cliffs as Dana promised herself she would stop Dahut with all she had. Her grace shot magnificently from her hand and met with Dahut's own black magic as the two beams countered each other – as a rock meets a hard place – the one with the strongest will, she knew, would win. The stalemate of power continued for several minutes.

"You can't defeat me!" Dahut shouted. "I finally have the power I seek. The power of a God! Whatever strength you have is nothing compared to my own!" Dahut emboldened her electrical blast, yet Dana countered.

"This strength is my own!" Dana shouted. "Yours is stolen. I've been fighting like this my entire life – and I won't give up now!"

Dana's grace outclassed Dahut's power, and as Dahut was about to be engulfed in it, she ordered the people of Ys to act. Suddenly, a group of them snuck up behind Dana and tackled her to the ground and began to beat her. The mermaids started to come to

Dana's aid, yet Dahut shocked them, paralyzing them in place. Now unmatched, she continued her attack on Ru and threw an explosive lightning bolt towards him, knocking him off balance, and forcing him under. As the giant rush of water started its way to Ys once more, Dahut turned her attention to Dana, "Now to finish you off, once and for all!"

Just as Dahut raised her electrical palm to kill Dana, something in the distance from below, came echoing up from the depths of the ruins, a sound that hadn't been heard in a decade. A chiming of bells, so beautiful and elegant, yet sad and homely. As holy and humble as they could be – the carillon of Ys reverberated with a might that shook the hearts of all the denizens of Ys. Their carved-out hollowed hearts and perverted and corrupted minds - became clear of the evil magic that influenced them, and instantly they fell to the ground in guilt. Lost in regret and feeling their sins, hopelessness riddled them. To face their souls after so long and after so many evils, tore them. Dana could see this all quite clearly as the people who were beating her quickly relinquished her and began to fiercely apologize in tears. Dana looked up to her sister, hoping for a similar change.

"This means nothing," Dahut spoke. "I'll just kill you all now."

And just as she was about to strike, King Mordred came running out from the shadows and stood between the two sisters. Dana had completely forgotten that he was amidst the people fighting as well.

"Stop this at once, Dahut!" The king shouted. He seemed more lucid now than ever in the last ten years. "Please, stop it! Please don't hurt her. Not your sister -"

Dahut did not hesitate. The lightning leapt from her fingers and shocked his body, so he was flung onto his back near Dana.

"F-father!" Dana scrambled to him. She could see only a little life left in him, yet his eyes were no longer clouded. He, like the others, had been freed from Dahut's curse. He looked up at her and held his hand out to her face. Dana grabbed the frail hand and pulled it to her cheeks.

"Dana… I am so sorry. I was so lost. So confused. But I see now the truth. You are such a wonderful daughter. I'm so very proud of you. You've done it, dear; you've freed us all. Oh, you look so much like your…mother. If only I had been strong enough for the both of you."

"Father, no!"

His hand fell from her and his eyes closed. "My people…" He spoke to those surrounding him and Dana, "My last order as your King – protect my daughter!"

"Father!" Dana sobbed.

"I…love…you." And the king's crown fell from his temple.

The denizens of Ys fearlessly charged Dahut, who, despite her great power, seemingly felt great fear when seeing the overwhelming conviction of a united people seeking a just cause; her death. Since her electricity was not enough to stop the horde of people, she sprouted bat-like wings to fly away in a final bid to escape.

"Stop her!" Dana commanded her people as she stood up. "At once!" The group quickly tackled Dahut, and despite being shocked one after another, they managed to tear the wings from her body. As she screamed in agony, Dana commanded her people once more, "leave her to me!"

The group scuttled away, and with a new conviction, with the love from her father in her heart, she finally found the confidence and power to overcome her sister. Dana pulsated with a golden glow that repelled all Dahut's attacks. The evil princess expelled all her hatred in a fantastical lightning blow, but it was to no avail. Through her tears, Dana fought valiantly, and with every step forward, she came closer and closer to her sister until, eventually, she put her hands upon her.

Dahut, surprised, ceased her futile attack as the two looked each other in the eyes. She tried to step back only to find that she had been pushed to the very edge of the dock and all that was below her was a deathly fall. She returned to her sister's gaze and, with a sneer, said, "you don't have it in you." Dana pushed with all her might, and Dahut fell backwards into the city below. She couldn't bear to watch her sister hit the ground. Her screams were enough.

Before Dana could process what had just happened, the thundering clash of water shook the ground beneath, causing everyone to fall over onto themselves.

Ru had succeeded, but at a deadly price. He managed to reject enough of the water so that it didn't flood the tower, but as a result, and because of Dahut's doing, he was hit by the massive wave and drowned underneath it. Dana crawled over to the beached dragon, as it lay motionless and breathless, and kissed it. She fell into grief. The people of Ys had been saved, yet she was without her friends and family. And then there was Ru, who was more than that…

The people and mermaids of Ys felt immense shame and sadness. They realized that he, the Son of God, had died for them, so that they could live. They felt responsible and joined Dana in her grief.

"Stop!"

Peter shouted loudly and grabbed everyone's attention. Dana looked up surprised. She thought the flood had engulfed him. "Peter? You're alive?"

"It was Enoch," Peter said as he ran up to her. "He teleported me here just in time. It would take too long to explain. It was an angel. Listen, he told me something I had forgotten. He told me to remember that to give something you must take away as well." Peter spoke louder so that all the people around could hear him. "Everyone! All hope is not lost. We must pray. We must have faith in God. If we offer Him some of our own lives to give to Ru, then perhaps he will return!"

The people murmured amongst themselves, questioning Peter's theory. Dana did not hesitate. On the very cliff where, as a child, she once prayed to God for the salvation of her people in exchange of her life, she was now doing for a single man. She put her palms together and prayed intently, offering a bit of her life for Ru's. She glowed intensely and that light stemmed onto the corpse before her. Peter then joined, and he also glowed with a light that was shared with the dragon's body. The people of Ys and the mermaids followed suit until all of Ys lit the dragon with a fierce radiance causing the red clouds in the sky to part, revealing the sun. The body, illuminated by the soft, white light surrounding it, began to elevate. It shrunk in size as it returned to Ru's original human body and he landed on his feet, eyes wide-open.

"Thank you," Ru said. "Thank you, everyone. You can stop praying now. Lift your heads."

Dana stood up and quickly jumped to him, hugging him in tears. "Ru…" She said between sobs, "I thought…you were dead!"

"I'm sorry, Dana. I won't ever leave you again," he said with a smile.

From the horizon, a gentle, yet commanding voice echoed, "my Son, my people. I have done you wrong. Your prayers and actions have shown me there is indeed hope and grace to be found in you, with a little guiding hand. With enough faith you are capable of greatness. You have all truly opened my eyes. I promise to never harm you again. I will never leave you, my children. Together and forever, we will flourish."

"Thank you, Father," Ru replied.

"Ru," God continued, "I offer you this. You are welcome to join me and reign over the universe, my Son. You may come with me now, back to your home in Heaven. Or you can stay, but in return I must take away your divinity. I cannot allow a God amongst men for long. Free will is part of mankind's journey and having a God among them would influence them, taking away their freedom of choice."

Ru looked down to Dana and then to Peter and all of the people behind him and replied, "I'm sorry, Father. But I'm needed here. I think I need them more than they need me. I'm not ready to give them up. I'll see you again when my time comes. But I have a life that I want to live…" Ru looked intently into Dana's eyes and she felt herself blushing.

"I understand… Remember, people of Ys, this one final lesson. To be divine or to be fallen… The choice is yours. But before I leave, there is one last thing…"

The mermaids began to shimmer, and their flaky, scaly skin returned to its former fleshy, human state. The water below that drowned the great city of Ys receded once more, and a giant rainbow painted the sky with beauty and promise. Ru held Dana closely and said to her, "I love you."

And she looked up at him and said, "I love you, too."

The two kissed and all of Ys rejoiced.

THE END

ABOUT THE AUTHOR

S.C. Vincent is an American author of Fantasy, Horror, and Science Fiction.

A NOTE FROM THE AUTHOR

Thank you for reading my book. If you enjoyed it, please consider leaving a review.

Follow my social media accounts here: https://linktr.ee/scvincent

OTHER WORKS BY S.C. VINCENT

The Arcadian Destiny

www.ingramcontent.com/pod-product-compliance
Lightning Source LLC
LaVergne TN
LVHW021817060526
838201LV00058B/3416